MW01166679

20 short ones

20 Short Stories

Dan Salerno

WestBow Press books may be ordered through booksellers or by contacting:

WestBow Press
A Division of Thomas Nelson
1663 Liberty Drive
Bloomington, IN 47403
www.westbowpress.com
1-(866) 928-1240

ISBN: 978-1-4908-0580-1 (sc)
ISBN: 978-1-4908-0581-8 (e)

Printed in the United States of America.

Library of Congress Control Number: 2013914950

WestBow Press rev. date: 12/04/2013

Cover by Roger Heldt

Table of Contents

Agee

It all started when Agee was walking home from school, as he passed an apartment building close to the corner. Waiting for the light to change, Agee glanced up and noticed a piece of paper drifting down from an open window. It was snow white and he snatched it as it swirled around him. There was a message written on it: "I'm tired. Good-bye. 4B."

Agee was thinking: Why would someone bother to write a note and not even sign it? And to top it off, why would they toss it out the window? He was thinking this when he heard the gunshot coming from the same open window.

Although he was relatively young at eight years old, Agee could put two and two together. He figured there had to be some sort of connection between the note and the gunshot and the police would probably want what he was now clutching in his hand for evidence. So, he calmly walked across the street to the doorman who had been inside the lobby during all this and hadn't a clue.

"Where'd you get this?" the doorman asked.

"Someone in your building wrote it and it floated down to me," said Agee.

Within two minutes the paramedics had arrived and had gained access to Edie's apartment, which was 4B. Luckily the person living in 4C was home and had heard the shot and the subsequent thud of someone falling against the wall and onto the floor. Luckier still, Edie didn't know how to fire a pistol properly and had aimed far enough away from her head to only graze it.

When the emergency room doctor asked Edie why she tried to kill herself, she smiled as if embarrassed and told her: "I was having a bad day, that's all."

The next day Agee heard about it when the doorman motioned him over for a chat on his way home from school. "Kid, you saved her life."

"What do you mean?"

"When the cops came to talk to her in the ER, she said it was an accident. But the note she wrote that you found proves there was intent to do bodily harm. So instead of letting her go, the doctors sent her to the psych ward at Our Lady of Angels for observation."

Feeling somewhat responsible, Agee asked Susan (his mother, who wasn't the type to pry into anyone's business) if he could visit Edie, which meant that she had to call the hospital, explain the situation, and accompany him.

Once they got to the psych ward, Susan stayed in the waiting room while her son was escorted down the hall to the social room. Edie was sitting on a couch, looking intently at a replica of Van Gogh's *Starry Night.* Very used to engaging adults in conversation, after being pointed in the right direction, Agee went up to Edie and introduced himself.

"Hi. I'm the guy who found your note."

"What?"

"I found your note. Actually, it floated out your window right to me."

Edie was 36 years old, brown-eyed with auburn hair that was cut short with a layered look. She was five-foot-three and worked for a theatre group as a marketing director. Normally she wore oval shaped glasses with black rims. But at the minute she wasn't wearing them. They were in the pocket of her hospital gown because she was farsighted and didn't particularly want to remember any details of the hospital.

"Yeah, well, thanks for nothing."

"Pardon?" Agee was a very literal minded person and he had no idea why this woman would thank him for doing nothing.

"The note. I wasn't being honest...you should have just ignored it..." Almost instantly Edie caught herself, despite the situation. She held out her hand. "I'm sorry. My name's Edie. What's yours?"

"Agee."

"Agee, like the playwright?"

"So I'm told."

Edie couldn't help laughing. "What a grown-up way of putting it."

"Putting what?"

"The fact that you know that you're named after a famous writer."

"Lots of people are named after someone or something. How about you?"

"I'm not one of those people."

Actually Edie was one of those people. Her mother was 19 years old when she gave birth without the benefit of knowing, for sure, who the father was. She chose the name for her daughter because out of the blue she was thinking of names that rhymed with Stevie Nicks, the singer. If her daughter wouldn't have the benefit of knowing her dad, at least she'd know that her name was linked with someone whose history was traceable. Unfortunately, Edie hated Fleetwood Mac and that got in the way of appreciating Stevie Nicks. Anyway, she had her own definite taste in music and it didn't include any bands or solo acts from the 70's.

Being the sensitive sort, Agee tried to steer the conversation away from first names. "So, how long have you lived in your apartment building?"

"Not long, actually, only a few weeks. I used to live across town. I had a place close to my boyfriend, but he and I weren't getting along and I needed a change."

"You got tired of each other?"

"Tired?"

"Yeah, that's what you wrote on your note."

Edie took a deep breath. She had to make a quick decision. Why was this kid asking her such a direct question? What business of his was it? Did she want to expend the emotional energy it would take to explain? On the other hand, he was just a kid. A precocious one, but still, a kid. Should she go ahead and take a chance on the offhand that maybe this young boy, by engaging her in conversation, would draw out what was buried inside her? Or should she leave it up to the professionals?

Ultimately, she decided that it was just as easy to speak to Agee as to any credentialed adult about her personal business.

"I was very tired of the lies."

"How can lies make you tired?"

"It takes a lot of energy to keep telling them. That's the simplest way of putting it."

"So, you didn't want to live anymore?"

"No. Not exactly." To her genuine surprise, Edie found she wanted to explain herself. Especially to someone so young and inexperienced and untouched.

"You know how, when you feel really tired, sometimes you say things that you don't mean? Or you do things that, later on, when you're not tired, you feel sorry for doing?"

"Sure."

"Well, it was like that with my boyfriend and I. Not at first, but then it got like that, more and more until all we were doing was telling each other lies."

"That's terrible!"

"Yeah. It is terrible, isn't it?" Edie began to cry uncontrollably. Which wouldn't have attracted attention under normal circumstances, but she was in a psych ward, under observation, and she wasn't just crying, she was bawling her head off. The dam of three year's worth of frustration and pain had burst and there was no holding back.

Agee instinctively pulled out a clean handkerchief and offered it to her.

"Please come back and see me, ok?"

Agee nodded as he was escorted out of the room.

That night, within seconds of his mother kissing him goodnight, Agee dreamed that he was weightless. The sensation, at first, was exhilarating, as he spread his arms up and caught a thermal. You know the feeling you get in your stomach when you're on a swing-set on a down-swing, right at the moment when you start to zoom up again? Well, multiply that by fifty zillion and that's what Agee was experiencing.

At first it was swell, he hadn't a care in the world. But little by little a feeling of pressure came over him. He was flying directly into a pack of polka-dotted birds with huge bright red beaks who kept on squawking: "Keep it to yourself! Keep it to yourself!" as they spit needles at him. Pretty soon, Agee's body felt like a balloon let go, with all of the air rushing out causing it to go into a tailspin.

The next day being Saturday, Agee was able to go back to the hospital with his mom in the morning. When he found Edie again sitting in the social room, she made eye contact and waved him over.

"I'm so glad you came back!"

Agee didn't quite know what to make of that opening, but he figured he'd give Edie the benefit of the doubt and let it slide.

"Hi."

"So, I was thinking how do lies begin anyway?"

"What?" Agee wasn't prepared for any questions, but the subject interested him.

"I mean, how do we even begin to lie in the first place? It's not like anyone has to teach us."

"It's original sin," said Agee, matter-of-factly.

For some reason, Edie thought that was absolutely hilarious. She began pealing with laughter but stopped when she saw the look on Agee's face.

"Sorry about that. But you sound so sure of yourself. Like a pint-sized preacher."

"You don't have to be a preacher to know about sin."

"You're right. It's just that I haven't spent a whole lot of time inside any house of worship."

Agee's mom was Jewish. Susan had grown up going to a reformed synagogue, but after getting pregnant she decided to hedge her bets and raise her son to believe in the triune God. She went along with Pascal's dilemma, taking it to the next level. Even if you don't believe in God's Son, there's no hurt in living as if He had one. If it turns out He didn't, you've lived a moral life. If it turns out He did, then you're gotten yourself safely home. Either way, no harm done.

Agee had grown up with this understanding and voluntarily read the Bible and attended Sunday School taught by a small, non-denominational church around the corner from the apartment he shared with his mother, who was excited to see her son actively pursuing his spiritual development.

"You're upset because you and your boyfriend were telling each other lies? That's why you wrote that message?"

Edie was more than willing to explain herself. Other than her recent engagement with a team of mental health therapists, she hadn't had a decent conversation in years, so her pump was primed. In a flash, she thought back to how difficult it had been growing up to have a genuine talk with anyone her own age. School had pretty much been a disaster. She learned early on in the transition from middle school to high school that she didn't fit into any of the established cliques. She didn't start really dating until college and by then she'd become so used to thinking on her own that didn't stop to consider the benefits of having someone else's input. But now, all of a sudden, as long as she seemed to be free-falling, she figured: What the heck, two days ago I put a gun to my head, what have I got to lose?

"Well, now that you mention it, I am angry," she said, looking into Agee's eyes, as if to anchor her thoughts.

"I'm angry at my boyfriend for wasting my time and not caring enough to tell the truth. I'm angry at him for fooling me into caring about him enough to deliberately live within walking distance of his apartment. Most of all I'm angry for not being honest with myself."

"So, actually you're mad at yourself then?"

"Angry and disappointed and frustrated."

"I've never met anyone who was so angry that they wanted to hurt their own self."

Agee wasn't planning on it, but he told Edie about Susan. How, his first memories of his mom were of her sitting on the windowsill of their apartment, looking outside and sighing. How he would fall asleep lulled by her muted crying coming from the next room. She had thought she was sparing her son from being part of the tragedy of a broken heart, and in a way, she was. Instead of any bitterness, what Agee remembered was the softness of lingering pain. Susan wasn't a complainer, and she had always thought that her son was a blessing. There had never been a doubt about that. Such devotion held no room for judgment.

"So your mom never spoke to you about your dad?"

"She didn't know who my dad was."

"Wow. Your mom told you that?"

"Yes," said Agee matter-of-factly. "When I was having my fourth birthday, I asked her and she told me."

"Straight out, just like that?"

"Pretty much." It wasn't that the subject of his potential father was difficult, but, at the minute, Agee was much more interested in Edie than in himself. "What about your boyfriend? Does he know you're in here?"

Edie took a good look at Agee, smiled and let out what could only be described as a roar of a laugh. You know the type, with your head tilted back and tears coming down your face.

"Well, first of all, I have to tell you, he's not my boyfriend any longer. There's not much of an incentive for me to get in touch with him, you know? I mean, bang-bang and all that." (Edie put a finger to her head for emphasis.)

Agee nodded, realizing that she had just begun to scratch the surface.

"He and I weren't exactly into telling each other the truth. I mean, what's the point of hanging out with someone who brings out the worst in you?"

"I get your point."

Edie was wondering just how far she wanted to go in describing her relationship with her now defunct boyfriend. Should she talk about the terrible emptiness that eventually all lies lead to? Should she talk about how lying became addictive, just as addictive as heroin, just as destructive? Just as necessary to get through the day? That in the end, the temporary relief didn't diminish the longing for truth? She wondered how much of this Agee would be able to understand. She decided that his visits had actually forced her to consider all this, much more than any group therapy sessions she was attending as part of her current treatment.

"You know, the older you get the harder it is to tell the truth sometimes," she said, deciding to take a chance and broach the subject.

"Why is that?"

"Life gets complicated. As soon as you begin understanding that there's more to life than you, and become interested in other people, then you realize you can't live without them, and you stop telling the truth so that they'll like you."

"No kidding!" Agee was genuinely surprised by this piece of information. "So, you had to stop telling the truth so that you could have friends?"

"Well, now that you put it that way, yes, it does make a lot of sense. People realize they need to be loved, right? So, part of the price you pay for love is to turn a blind eye to what could hurt somebody."

Agee thought about the times that his mom would pick up

the phone, start to dial, let it ring once or twice and then gently put the receiver down. Then there were other times when she would sit and look at the phone, as if she had the power to cause someone on the other end to phone her. When Agee would ask her if anything was wrong, his mom would look at him, smile and say, "No, sweetie, everything's fine."

"But why have friends if you can't tell them the truth? I thought the whole idea was to be able to share secrets?"

Edie raised her eyebrows just a tad before replying. "In theory that's the way it should work, but a lot of the time it just doesn't pan out."

"So you decided to stop trusting your friends and kept your secrets to yourself?"

"It was more like I decided not to get to the place where I had any secrets."

Agee was genuinely impressed. "You must have had amazing self control."

"Actually, it was easy once I decided that nothing mattered."

This was truly interesting. Agee had heard about people who didn't believe in anything. Or said that they didn't believe in anything. But he had never met anyone in his eight-year-old life who said that nothing mattered.

"So, to have a secret, it has to matter to you in the first place?"

"Exactly."

Instantly Agee flashed back to his mom again. He understood why she had never spoken about his dad, other than to say that he had one. There was no secret. Nothing to share. But Edie's lack of secrets sprang from a different source.

"You must have built up a whole ocean full of memories behind you."

"Why would you say that?" Edie was now the one who was curious.

"Because everybody has experiences that they need to tell

other people about. If they don't they just stay there and build up until they're shared with someone."

Who was this kid, thought Edie. And why am I in the mood to listen to what he's telling me? What does a little peewee like him know anyway? He hasn't had a girlfriend lie to him. He hasn't had to face the embarrassment that comes from sharing special memories with the wrong person. On the other hand thought Edie, maybe this kid is on to something. Maybe love trumps embarrassment. Maybe that's what Shakespeare meant.

"'It's better to have loved in vain than never to have loved at all'" said Agee.

You could have knocked Edie over with a spoon. "Where did you learn that?"

"I have a pretty good memory for a catchy phrase and I take an accelerated English class."

"You don't say!"

Agee slowly held out his hand to hold Edie's.

It was a very subtle gesture, but then most things that last begin like that.

Mercy

*"And what does the Lord require of you?
To act justly and to love mercy and to walk
humbly with your God."*

—Micah 6:8 (New International Version)

Mercy was 15 when her sister died after being hit by a drunk driver. The judge's decision had been 'under the influence,' which is an interesting way of putting it. She remembered very clearly sitting in the courtroom, and the gasp from the driver's mother before she openly started to weep. As far as Mercy was concerned, it was legalistic histrionics. She decided, then and there, that her dream of one day becoming a trial lawyer was a waste of time. Besides, did winning the case for the prosecution bring her sister back to life? She was still dead, no matter what had been decided.

Five years later she was beginning her senior year in college. By that time Mercy had spent two years ruling out other majors like bio-chemistry, physics, all of the other sciences, and the in-between stuff like history and art, before settling on English literature, in particular, the Romantic poets. She loved sitting down to breakfast with guys like Samuel Taylor Coleridge while munching on Rice Krispies:

"A damsel with a dulcimer
In a vision I once saw;
It was an Abyssinian maid,
    And on her dulcimer she played,
Singing of Mount Abora.
Could I revive with me
Her symphony and song,
To such a deep delight 'twould win me,
That with music loud and long,
I would build that dome in air,
That sunny dome! Those caves of ice!
    And all who heard should see them there,
And all should cry Beware! Beware!
His flashing eyes, his floating hair!
Weave a circle round him thrice,
And close your eyes with holy dread,
For he on honey-dew hath fed,
And drunk the milk of Paradise."

(Heaven only knows what sort of anodyne Sammy boy had ingested to get him so pumped up.)

Besides the benefit of such wistful meanderings, no one who held an interesting job was hiring English Lit majors. So you might as well have some incredible verse to mull over in your mind to feed the imagination. Actually, Mercy had planned ahead and gotten an internship at the local Boys & Girls Club, heading up an after-school mentoring program.

It was there, on an uncharacteristically sunny March afternoon, that she sat across the table from Tilley, a precocious 11-year-old who had asked to see her.

"What's up, Til?"

Tilley sat there, staring into space like she was watching the weather channel when the whole nation was experiencing a rainy day. She was most definitely in a different time zone.

"Earth to Tilley!"

"Huh?"

"You wanted to see me?"

Mercy was thinking: It was too bad that she couldn't just reach out and give a kid an emotional massage to help them get over whatever was bothering them inside. But experience had shown her that it was best to take your lead from the child and let them make the first move.

"I guess so."

Guess so? This wasn't like Tilley. She was one of the most outgoing, positive kids at the Club. She was always engaged with a group; helping the younger ones to feel at home and looking out for the first-timers who came in from the neighborhood, fresh off the street, a little rough around the edges.

"Would you like half a ham sandwich? I was just getting ready to have lunch. What do you say?"

Tilley sat up and gave a small piece of a smile. Whoever first quipped that a way to a man's heart was through their stomach wasn't too far off. Except that it wasn't just for guys. Most everyone liked to eat.

"Sure. I could go for that. Thanks."

Mercy opened up her sack lunch, took out the sandwich and handed half of it over to Tilley.

"So, are you going to try out for the track team? That's coming up next week."

"I don't think so."

"You are one of the fastest runners in this place! It'd be a shame if you didn't."

"I just don't feel like it."

"Wow. That's like a duck saying that it just doesn't feel like getting in the water!"

"What?"

"Ducks love water Til. In fact, they can't survive without it. They get most everything they need from it. A bath, food, companionship with other ducks. Quack! Quack!" She reached out and gave Tilley a gentle push on the shoulder, which got her to open up her smile a bit.

"Cut it out."

"Cut what out?"

"The silly stuff. You're just trying to get me to laugh."

Mercy feigned surprise as she put her palm hard across her forehead.

"You mean it isn't working?"

Tilley's smile grew wider. "No."

"Are you absolutely sure?"

"Yes."

"Til, are you messing with me?"

She tried to stifle a giggle, but it wasn't working.

"No."

"Scouts honor?"

Out it came. Loud and clear. Tilley was ready to talk now.

"I've been thinking about something. That's why I wanted to see you."

"O.K."

"I want to know why my dad left before I was even born. What did I do?"

Instinctively Mercy moved a bit closer to Tilley, trying to protect her.

"Tilley, you didn't do anything. You weren't even there when he went away."

"But my mom told me last night it wasn't like that."

"What do you mean?"

"She said that if I hadn't been born, my dad would have stayed. But I was a worthless piece of baggage that he didn't want to deal with."

Tilley's mom was known to occasionally push the suds when she was feeling under it. She had mentioned it to Mercy a few times, almost casually; usually the morning after her mom had been drinking.

"You know that what she said isn't true!"

Tilley shook her head. "But it feels like it is."

"Has your mom told you other things like that?"

"Usually when she's been drinking she's just plain mad at everyone. But last night was different. She was crying in her room and so I went in there to find out what was going on. The door was wide open. I found her sitting on the floor, and there was a box of pictures thrown all over the place, but she was holding onto one of them and staring at it."

"Did you see the picture?"

"Yeah. It was my mom with my dad, sitting on a park bench and smiling. I'd seen it before. But she was staring at it and crying. When I asked her what was wrong, that's when she told me I was baggage. I had no idea she felt that way. I mean, when she's had a few she's a different person, but she'd never acted this way towards me before."

"Tilley, I am so sorry that your mom said those things to you. She didn't really mean them. You've got to understand, she wasn't being herself. She was in a very bad place and you just happened to interrupt her."

"Well, it was a complete accident on my part. Why do people have to be so angry when they get interrupted?"

"In your mom's case, I don't know the answer. Usually we filter out thoughts that aren't nice so we don't speak them. But sometimes, people get in a place where the filter isn't working."

"Tell me about it!"

"So they need help because they really aren't thinking clearly at that point."

From out of nowhere Mercy's memory called to mind *The Merchant of Venice.* You know the part where Portia, disguised as a lawyer is pleading with Shylock to get him to reconsider cutting a pound of flesh off Antonio for defaulting on a debt? She approaches the judge and says:

"The quality of mercy is not strain'd
It droppeth as the gentle rain from heaven

Upon the place beneath. It is twice blest;
It blesseth him that gives and him that takes."

The point is that that you can't force a person to be merciful, because it's based on grace. But once given, mercy blesses both the one who gives it as well as the one who's fortunate to receive it.

"What am I supposed to do, then?" asked Tilley, bringing Mercy back to the moment.

"You basically have a choice. If you extend some mercy to your mom, you might just wind up helping her out of a difficult place."

"What's the other choice?" Tilley wasn't exactly eager to make a decision on this one without exploring the other option.

"You can demand to take a pound of flesh."

"You aren't making any sense."

"I mean, it's a Merchant of Venice type situation. Your mom has broken an unspoken promise to protect you and always defend you, no matter what. So, you can either grant her mercy and forgive her, or else you can demand your rights as her kid and cut off a pound of flesh emotionally, and hurt her back by cutting her off from your heart."

Tilley was silent for a minute as she thought it through in her 11 year old mind. The first option didn't really make a lot of sense at the minute. So she was seriously considering going the second route. Until something struck her as odd.

"If I cut off my mom, then she can't ever hurt me again. But I also won't be able to love her as strongly as I do right now. I mean, something's got to give. And isn't it true that no matter who you choose to love, they can always choose not to love you back? Or even worse, they could hurt you?"

"Unfortunately, that's right."

"So that's just the way life is. You either hole up somewhere so you won't get hurt, or else you're out there, laying it on the line. I mean within reason."

"Pretty much, that's the way it goes." Mercy was impressed with Tilley's ability to figure this sort of a thing out at such a young age.

"What would you do?"

"Til, it doesn't matter what I'd do. It's up to you. It's your mom we're talking about and it's your life. I wish I could keep you from getting hurt again, but I can't."

Tilley looked down and put her hands on her head.

All of a sudden, Mercy was 15 again. She was back in the courtroom. This time when the judge handed down the decision, and the drunken driver's mother began to sob uncontrollably, it wasn't legalistic histrionics. What Mercy saw was a mother of a teenaged son crying in recognition of what her child had done. Mercy still realized that the boy had been driving under the influence. She still recognized that her sister's life ended. She still felt the pain of that loss. But this time, she understood that other people, outside of her own family, had been affected by the boy's actions. A mother was forced to deal with the unfathomable grief that her son had caused. And for the first time, she remembered looking into the mother's eyes to see the deep sorrow there. Mercy could no longer retain the resentment she had always felt towards the boy and his mother. And in that moment, sitting across the table from Tilley, she chose to release those feelings and forgive.

Another piece of poetry came into Mercy's mind, this one straight from Psalm 85:

> "Mercy and truth have met together,
> Righteousness and peace have kissed."

After a while Tilley sat straight up. She looked directly at Mercy before picking up the conversation.

"Life sure is complicated, isn't it?"

Mercy nodded.

"My mom has a drinking problem."

Mercy nodded again.

"Sometimes it causes her to get things messed up in her mind. She's had a bunch of broken relationships and she's carrying around a boatload of disappointment."

"Break-ups don't come easy."

"When it feels like your ship is sinking, it's easier to blame someone else as you're going down with the ship."

"It's a very lonely way to go."

"But I'm not my mom and I have a choice. I can choose to look beyond the ship, and when she yells at me because she's sinking and afraid, I can reach out my hand to her and offer her my love. Because I'm not on the same sinking boat if I make that choice."

Where does love come from? Is it somehow connected to forgiveness? And does that mean that the ultimate source of both of these gifts is outside of us? Mercy looked into Tilly's eyes and saw something there that had been missing when their conversation began only a few minutes ago.

"Til, that's quite a lot for a young person to understand. Are you sure you're really getting this?"

Tilly slowly nodded 'yes.' "Hard things either strengthen you or kill you, and one thing I know, I'm not a weakling."

Pleasure

Yvonne was minding her own business when all of a sudden a memory shot itself up from her subconscious. She was 15, and on a trip with her mom to the big city. Chicago, to be exact. They had taken a train in for the day from Michigan City.

It had been typical Midwestern June weather – warm and sunny and just perfect for taking a hike to Grant's Park from Union Station. As they got into the Park to find a bench to settle in for some people watching, they walked right by Buckingham Fountain where a couple was kissing, completely oblivious to anyone else.

Good night, thought Yvonne. Get a room or something! Her next thought was spawned by simple and complete awe: How in the world could two people seem to be having so much enjoyment with each other?

Yvonne wasn't thinking this because of sexual ignorance. She knew what was what. She had the "birds and the bees" talk with an older cousin three years before and Yvonne had actually told her cousin a thing or two. I mean, kids grow up so quickly, don't they?

Yvonne knew all about the physical aspects of pleasure. What she didn't understand was why certain actions seemed to elicit such intensity. And it wasn't just sex. It was everything. For instance: Why were most people able to laugh out loud at jokes, when the best she could muster up was a smile? Why did some people seem to take delight in walking outside during a summertime shower to get absolutely soaking wet? Why did others take immense joy in hanging out with their friends, talking about nothing in particular?

In ninth grade Yvonne had gone to a school dance on a Friday night. She wasn't exactly looking forward to it. So when she walked into the gym and saw most of the kids there standing within their own social cliques, having animated conversations, and very few couples actually dancing, she immediately turned on her heels, headed towards the door and walked home. Along the way, she was wondering how a person could think such a thing was fun?

"I don't get it. I really don't get it," she had said on the way home that evening.

And it wasn't as if she was depressed. At least not clinically. Sure, there were days when Yvonne felt down, but mostly, her emotions were on the positive side. For instance, she was the first one to admit that a sunrise or sunset was beautiful. She enjoyed the smell of a pine forest, and how the trees all seemed to line up in straight rows. But she didn't feel the need to get all worked up about it.

Then there was the time in the Student Union bathroom in college.

She had sat there on the toilet for a good 20 minutes after feeling a little anxious. It was the day before Christmas break, and there was a constant stream of coeds going back and forth, mostly in groups, laughing, on their way to burning off a little steam after studying way too long. Yvonne too was grateful that her finals were over. But being surrounded by so many students who were clearly ecstatic made her anxious. So she went to the bathroom and sat on the toilet. The bathroom stalls were a welcome sanctuary when other public spaces were taken.

Maybe I have a guy's emotional outlook trapped inside a girl's body, she had thought, trying to figure out some of the graffiti on the cubicle wall in front of her. Or maybe this isn't an emotional thing at all. It's a question of personality, the whole introvert vs. extrovert dilemma. Yvonne had taken some psych courses and had remembered classroom discussion about theories of how personhood is established. A combination of environment, parental influence and DNA coming together to produce a unique individual.

So, here she was now, grown up, sitting on the front steps of the Art Institute of Chicago. All around her was the hustle and bustle of the holidays. She was an assistant curator, having worked there for seven years. And she was sitting outside to get a breath of fresh air before heading back to the Impressionists section which was her responsibility.

"I could use an epiphany," she said, not realizing she had spoken the words out loud, attracting the attention of Martin Bloomfield, who happened to be walking by at that moment, on his way inside.

"Pardon?" he said.

"Excuse me?" she replied.

"You just said that you could use an epiphany." Martin worked as a research assistant at the Sun-Times, so naturally his job trained him to be focused on the facts. Outside of work, however, was a different matter for the 30-year-old who took the bus in from Elk Grove every morning. Outside of work, he reveled in spontaneity and had a quick wit and easy smile.

"I'm sorry. I had no idea I actually spoke that out loud."

"So, why do you want an epiphany?"

She felt herself turning red. "It's sort of personal."

"I know, but you've got my curiosity going. Want to grab a cup of coffee in the cafeteria?" he motioned towards the door.

Yvonne looked at her watch, which was a normal reaction. Her second reaction should have been to make up an excuse, but instead what came out of her mouth was: "I've got my lunch break coming up. Can I get back to my office for a few minutes, and meet you there?"

Martin nodded and they both went inside. Less than ten minutes later they were sitting across from each other. He began the formalities.

"I don't mean to pry, but what you said out there intrigued me. I work at the Sun-Times and my job is nothing but checking assumption against reality. In theory, I try to keep the newspaper honest."

She raised her eyebrows. "I can see where that might be several people's full time occupation."

Yvonne hadn't meant to be sarcastic, but the statement had the effect of making Martin laugh.

"I guess I had that coming, huh?"

"No, no, no, please I didn't mean it that way. It was just a statement, that's all."

She wished that she could get up and leave, without having to explain why. Without having to sludge through another conversation void of feeling.

"How about if we skip the small talk and get back to the epiphany. Would that be easier?"

"Actually, it would." Yvonne sighed in relief "I was thinking about how most people seem to sail through life, socially I mean, with seemingly little effort. They grow up being exposed to a lot of different people and situations that cause them to have fun. But I didn't have that."

"Didn't have what?"

"The privilege of having parents who were social together. Or having two parents, period. Outside of my grandparents, we never went to anyone's house as a family."

She was the oldest of four. Two girls and two boys, born almost exactly two years apart from each other. For a period of time, as a young girl, all she could remember was her mom being continually pregnant. Yvonne was the proverbial big sister, learning how to change diapers at three years of age. She knew the logistics of being a mother very well, which, looking back on it, may have been a contributing factor to her lack of interest in dating. Even before she could articulate it, she knew that boys were somehow responsible for at least half of making a baby. And her experience had taught that some boys don't stick around to see the project through. Case in point, her father, who had up and left his wife and four young children when Yvonne was eight. Right after the last sibling was born. In fact, he had gone to the grocery store the day after bringing the new addition to the family home, and never came back.

"Your parents split up then?"

"Yeah. How about your family?"

Martin had a twin sister. They were close when growing up and remained that way. As for his parents, they ran a restaurant in Elk Grove for 32 years before retiring. It had been very much a family business, with Martin and his sister helping out after school once they reached sixth grade. They came straight home from school, did their homework, then headed to the restaurant a block away. After eating their supper there, they both pitched in to bus tables and work the dishwasher. It was hard work, but fun because the restaurant was a real neighborhood hangout and most everyone went there at some point to eat during the week.

"It was a lot of fun growing up. My family ran a restaurant. We knew all of the other families on our side of town. It was great."

Yvonne had no way to relate to that amount of socialization. "So that's where you learned how to make small talk?"

Martin smiled. "I didn't learn it. I just did it. People are people, and people like to talk, and so I listened and eventually started to join in the conversation."

"You enjoy doing that?"

"Sure, yeah. That's how you get to know people."

Martin's comment threw her for a loop. "No kidding."

"No. I'm not kidding."

She closed her eyes for a moment to center her thoughts before speaking. "In my experience, talking oftentimes gets in the way of communicating. The flow of ideas gets carried away in an ocean of chit-chat."

"But what you call chit-chat is just a way for people to break the ice. To become relaxed with each other so a real heart-to-heart can happen."

"Heart-to-heart?"

"Yes."

"I guess I've never experienced that."

Yvonne tried to think back to the last time she did something without planning. She drew a complete blank. One of the major reasons that she enjoyed working at the Art Institute was that everything was done according to schedule. Senior staff even had meetings about how to be more effective in their scheduling, where they cross-referenced each other's calendars. Nothing was done without purpose. Her social life, such as it was, seemed to follow the same pattern. She mostly met people from work after work for work-related discussions. As she looked at Martin she marveled at how he seemed to have found a way to blend work with fun, even from a young age. He seemed genuine and very likeable.

All of sudden a broad grin moved across Martin's face. "How would you like to meet me in the lobby of the Palmer House around six?"

If this had been an ordinary day, Yvonne would have grabbed her purse and bolted from the cafeteria, setting a personal best in getting the heck out of Dodge. But she picked up on Martin's confidence and allowed herself to feel a smidgen of safety in his company. Her intuition told her that his offer was nothing more than an invitation to have fun. But she still needed some assistance in getting outside of her comfort zone.

"You're serious?"

"Completely."

"What's the reason?"

"Do we have to have one?"

"I can't walk into the Palmer House off the street completely on a whim. It's too risky."

"Risky?"

Yvonne shook her head as if to clear her brain. "I'm really sorry, but if I don't have a good enough reason, I'll probably walk right by it and go home."

"How about pretending that we're strangers in the city and I just happened to see you from the second floor and couldn't help but notice you?"

Yvonne was flattered. "Honestly?"

Martin shook his head in the affirmative. "Is that good enough for you, to begin with?"

She stretched and stood up. "Yes."

He stuck out his hand, "Good, the name's Martin by the way."

"Yvonne. Thanks for the invitation."

The rest of the work day went by at a snail's pace. Normally she would have been extremely focused and happy to be back ensconced in her routine. Or she would have avoided the challenge of getting to know someone new by turning them down to begin with. But this time she gave herself permission to experience anticipation.

At 5:45 Yvonne walked through the Art Institute's front door and headed towards the Palmer House. Ten minutes later she was sitting on a very comfy chair, her heart racing. "It's really nothing, nothing at all," she tried to tell herself.

At six on the dot, Martin came into the lobby, and casually walked up to Yvonne, smiling. He had deliberately chosen to walk across her field of vision so that he wouldn't startle her from behind. He motioned to the chair next to her.

"Do you mind if I sit down?"

Yvonne shook her head no.

"I was standing by the side entrance and couldn't help but notice you. But then that's sort of a hokey way to begin a conversation, isn't it? I mean, in a place like this, I would guess that the doorman should check your suave credentials before they let people in."

She was pleasantly caught off guard and actually found herself wanting to smile.

"Well, I got in, so that's not saying much for suave security around here, is it?"

He had no problem laughing out loud.

"So are you from the city or visiting?"

Usually Yvonne would answer a straight question with a straight answer, but for some reason, she didn't feel at all like doing so. "I'm traveling with the circus."

Martin was quick on the uptake. "No kidding! What act?"

"I'm a trapeze artist. Maybe you've heard of Finkel and Feinstein?"

"Wow. That's a first. I have to say I've never heard of Jewish trapeze artists."

"Well, that's because my partner and I work for a special circus that has its roots in a Hasidic sect in Transylvania."

"So, you're married then?"

"Actually no. The Rebbe won't give his consent to such a blatant occasion to hang out with a bunch of Apikores. We sort of left the sect when the circus broke ranks and began to travel outside of Eastern Europe."

"That must have been very tough for you."

"It actually turned out to be quite a mitzvah. We were having a difficult time staying kosher living with all those cloven animals anyway. But enough about me, what's your line of work?"

Martin looked Yvonne directly in the eyes. "CIA, former FBI, former NSA. There aren't that many of us left."

Yvonne's heart wasn't pounding anymore. In fact, she felt strangely at ease. "How do you mean?"

"Well, with the most recent change in administration in Washington, the powers that be didn't want any operatives spilling their guts to the other intelligence branches, so a few of us were assigned to cross over under different covers."

"Wow, that must be very hard for you."

"I've had to completely vanish under false pretenses six times within two years. The CIA and FBI both thought I had gone rogue on them, which didn't help matters."

"How can you stand the pressure?"

"Grape Nuts."

"Pardon?"

"I eat a lot of Grape Nuts. It helps get out the aggression. But if you want to learn anything more, I'm afraid we'll have to do it over dinner."

"Where?"

"We'll have to go out the lobby door, turn right, and walk up two blocks to an Irish-Italian place that's safe. And it doesn't hurt matters that they make the best spaghetti and meat balls in the city. You aren't packing heat by any chance are you?"

"Not tonight."

As Yvonne got up and began to walk towards the door she gradually became aware that she was walking alongside of Martin. (She had developed a tendency to walk a half-step behind people.)

Then she noticed, as they turned right and headed up Monroe Street, how at ease she continued to feel. This wasn't at all what she was used to, but instead of throwing her for a loop, the realization confirmed her trust in him. And it was at that very instant, as she clasped her hand around Martin's, she smiled a smile that positively lit up her entire face.

"Are we having fun yet?" Martin asked mischievously.

"Absolutely," she said as she swung his arm high up in the air.

Silent Night

Before you go any further, you need to know that this story begins on December 16th. Not just any December 16th, but one where it was snowing, and the campus of Lovett College was covered in white for Christmas. All across the tiny campus co-eds were hunkered down in study clusters, wherever there was free space to review textbooks and lecture notes.

Abbie was among the students who had survived exam week on nothing but strong coffee and homemade Christmas cookies. The kind that are 97% sugar. She was about to walk outside Lovett's library to get some sorely needed fresh air. As she turned the corner walking past the Science section, she tripped and fell on her right side. Almost immediately a hand reached down to help her.

"Good grief this is so embarrassing!" she said as a kind hearted soul pulled her up. "I'm not normally this clumsy! Must be the caffeine."

"Don't worry about it. Are you ok?"

"Yes, I'm fine. Thanks."

"The name's Kyle Hoffman."

"Abbie Sanducci."

"So, this is probably a really out-there guess, but by any chance were you about to get out of this depository of human infirmity and stretch your legs?"

"Yeah. Yes. I mean, you can only study for so long and

then... woosh-a-rooni." Abbie made a motion of sweeping her right hand over her head.

Kyle laughed. "Woosh-a-whati?"

"Rooni. Woosh-a-rooni. You know, as in: I'm drowning in too much stimulation."

As it turns out, Abbie and Kyle were both seniors. His family was from the Northeast. Hers was from 20 miles away.

Abbie's family was strict Italian Roman Catholic. Not the Americanized version where you thumb your nose at the Pope and sit back in the pew on Sunday morning snickering at the priest every time he mentions "holy mother the church." She had been raised to actually appreciate the nuisances of tradition. She had two older brothers who made it their business to include Abbie in every pick-up game of basketball they ever played. Because of this, Abbie often spent long hours hitting the hoops, and by default, hanging out with boys as they discussed whatever was on their minds, eventually becoming oblivious to the fact that Abbie was a girl.

Kyle, on the other hand, wasn't particularly religious, having grown up with agnostic parents who encouraged their two sons to think for themselves. Kyle had little experience with the opposite sex. He had spent grade school getting ready for high school, and high school getting ready for college. He studied at least two hours a night during the school year and had been the editor of the high school newspaper and ran track, in between working for his father, who owned a shipping business in Brooklyn. You would have thought that, being a big city boy, Kyle's experience with girls would have been extensive, but it wasn't.

"So, would you like some company?" Abbie asked. She had gorgeous brown eyes and an equally gorgeous smile, and she was trying really hard to break the ice.

"How about if we cut through the quad and head towards town?"

"Ever had pizza at Barney's? I haven't eaten anything close to real food all week."

Lovett wasn't much of a village but Kyle knew next to nothing about it. True to form, he had spent practically all of his time on campus. The downtown consisted of three restaurants, a bar, two clothing stores and a post office along one street. The other main street had a coffee shop, the aforementioned pizza joint, a plumbing/hardware place and a grocery store.

"Pizza sounds good."

"So, what led you to Lovett College?" asked Abbie.

"My parents wanted me to get out of the East Coast to get an education."

"Isn't it usually the reverse? I mean, the Ivy League and all."

"My Dad has a thing against intellectual elitism and we couldn't afford Ivy League anyway. How about yourself?"

"Well, I hate to admit it, but I live almost a stone's throw away from here and the main reason I came to Lovett was because I got a free ride."

"No kidding!"

"Yep. I am living proof that studying hard and applying for obscure scholarships pays off."

"What scholarships?"

"The ones available to Italian girls who like earth science whose grandmothers have died."

Kyle laughed. "I'm sorry. I didn't mean any disrespect towards your grandmother."

"It's ok. Grandma died when I was a kid."

"You're Italian then?"

"Actually, I'm Sicilian on my Dad's side and Greek on my Mom's. How about yourself?"

Over a late dinner of vegetarian pizza with side salads, Kyle began to explain. "My grandfather on my Dad's side is a Hassidic Jew from Williamsburg. My mom is Lithuanian, first generation in this country."

"Wow! Excuse me for being potentially insensitive, but you don't seem like a guy who spent a lot of time hanging out at the synagogue. Or else you received a special dispensation from the rabbi so you could be sitting here with me eating pizza."

Kyle laughed. "My dad just wasn't into wearing the traditional dress or embracing the external trappings of devotion."

"So, no dreidels to play with at Hanukah?"

"No dreidels."

"But what about your Mom?"

"She was raised a Lutheran, but she figured that the 95 Theses were as much about intolerance as they were about anything else."

At any rate, because Abbie and Kyle's conversation was taking place in the middle of finals week, a 20 minute chat, allowing barely enough time to respond to questions while finishing up the pizza, was the extent of their first meeting.

But as it was, Abbie and Kyle had to get back to hitting the books. Regardless of their major cultural differences and upbringings, one thing they had in common was a respect for academics and time well spent.

Speaking of which, Catholics seem to be born with an inherent awareness of time. Maybe some of this trait has to do with their liturgical year – every Sunday is prescribed and taken care of. There is a proper place for every important Christian celebration. And a typical Catholic Mass said on a Sunday runs like clockwork. Less than 48 minutes from the priest and acolytes making their entrance until the priest gives the final blessing, pretty much guaranteed. Jews also have a reverence for time, but it expresses itself vertically. There are also seasons and events that are celebrated, all rooted in a remembrance of the Eternal One.

Two days later, after hitting the books for way too many hours, Abbie was crashed out on a library couch outside of the periodicals room. She had intended to take a quick break by scanning back issues of National Geographic but no sooner had she cracked opened the front page of the first issue than she fell fast asleep.

It wasn't a typical type of sleep either. It was the middle of the afternoon and her subconscious was working overtime to make up for too much factual information being considered. Abbie was dreaming that she was back in grade school at Saint Monica's. It was a gorgeous early May morning and the entire student assembly was parading across the front lawn of the church singing. "Oh Mary, we crown thee with blossoms today, Queen of the heavens, Queen of the May..."

All of the girls were dressed in the school uniform of white blouse with Peter Pan collar, navy blue skirt and black patent-leather shoes. Except Abbie, who was dressed in a rich teal wedding gown, complete with a train that had to be every bit of 15 feet long. She was heading up the tail end of the procession, handing out 8 by 10 glossies of herself that she had autographed "with love, Queen of the May."

All of this was quite disconcerting to Abbie, as in real life she had made a gargantuan effort to avoid attention being given to her. She had been blessed with a keen mind a quick wit and good looks, but she never openly called attention to any of that. And the toughest part of being athletic for her wasn't the long hours of practice; it was the fact that being so good, she normally ran across the finish line first. It wasn't like she wanted to; it was more like she simply couldn't help it.

To make matters a bit more interesting, Abbie was also prone to embarrass easily, turning beet-red in the process. So almost every time she was called upon in class and gave a startlingly thorough answer, her cheeks would turn crimson. Ditto whenever any boy would muster up the courage to ask her out on a date. It wasn't that Abbie was playing hard to get, she was genuinely disinterested in the concept of dating. So the invitation would inevitably wind up with a ruby-cheeked Abbie politely declining the offer, leaving the boy flustered and thinking she was either stuck up, or one of those savants who lacked social skills. Of course Abbie was neither of these, but she figured it was in her best interest to let it go rather than spend time explaining why she was philosophically opposed to high school dating. And truth be told, it was more of an "I can think of a thousand better ways to use my time," than "I don't like dating," sort of stance.

While Abbie was busy tripping down memory lane in her sleep, Kyle was finishing up his essay on John Keats' "Endymion." Most students would have focused on the opening lines:

"A thing of beauty is a joy forever:
It's loveliness increases; it will never
Pass into nothingness; but still will keep
A bower quiet for us, and a sleep
Full of sweet dreams, and health, and quiet breathing..."

Instead, he went for a section beginning with line 572:

"And then I feel asleep. Ah, can I tell
The enchantment that afterwards befell?
Yet it but a dream: yet such a dream
That never tongue, although it overteem
With mellow utterance, like a cavern spring,
Could figure out and to conception bring
All that I beheld and felt."

Funny that while Kyle was deep in pondering the sweet mysteries of sleep, Abbie was actually in the thick of experiencing it. And it was exactly at the instant that Abbie was transported back to St. Monica's that Kyle had chosen to get up from his Keats-driven musings to get a drink of water. The nearest water fountain in the library was directly across from where Abbie lay dozing. Usually she was a notoriously deep sleeper, but the sound of Kyle walking by roused her. As Kyle bent over to get a drink, his back towards her, Abbie opened her eyes and smiled at him.

"Hi" she offered. And he, being startled, spit out the water from his mouth, hitting a poster advertising the Final Exam Blow Out Sale at the campus book store. Ever the one to offer a quick apology, Abbie continued, "Didn't mean to startle you. I was taking a break and fell asleep."

"No problem."

"So how's tricks?"

"Tricks?"

"Yeah. You know, tricks!" Abbie made a motion of pulling a rabbit out of a hat. But Kyle had just been contemplating the relationship between the conscious and the unconscious and he wasn't quite in the groove of where her sense of humor wanted to take them.

The trouble was that Kyle had always been sort of a literal minded egg-head. It may seem like a contradiction, but in Kyle's case it wasn't. He had the ability to zero in and focus on the smallest of minutiae. He could take abstract thought to the moon and back, but he could also be amazingly practical when given half a chance. As a way to counteract all of this, God had given Kyle a huge sense of humor. His wasn't the rapid-fire, my-eyes-are-darting-all-over-the-map, spewing-out-quips-at- the-speed-of-light sort of thing. It was a very gentle, laid-back ability to appreciate the ironies of life.

During his first weekend on campus, a group of freshmen guys had decided to venture into town, and hang out. Having a grand total of $4.57 to spend on meals that week until his first Pell grant check came through, Kyle had politely declined. When pressed to come anyway, Kyle said he was trying to set a world's record for eating kosher while being surrounded by gentiles.

Abbie was thinking that for some strange reason Kyle didn't make her face turn red. In fact, she felt totally comfortable with him. Which was a major breakthrough. Kyle was thinking that Abbie was about the most beautiful creature he had ever met. But neither one was going to tell the other what they were thinking. Ordinarily it wouldn't have mattered who said what, but this conversation was talking place on December 18th, the last of the final exams were being taken the following day, followed by a two-week break for the holidays. And who knew when either one of them would soon have the guts to say what was romantically on their minds come the New Year?

Kyle had never told a girl that he liked her. What was the point? In his experience, if you acted interested, they wrote you off as being a puppy-dog. If you acted like you didn't care, they wrote you off for being stuck-up. And anyway, why bother setting yourself up for potential major heartache and distraction? Plus being in love with someone normally involved a pretty major time commitment, which was something that Kyle did not have a lot of, with every day being weighed down with the strain of trying to balance academics with a few extra-curriculars and work.

Not to mention that in addition to being a practical egg-head, Kyle was also a bit of a social klutz. His parents didn't exactly trip the light fantastic back home in Brooklyn. If you aren't out there observing how others interact, and do a little interacting yourself, you don't have much of a chance to mimic patterns of socially acceptable behavior, like dating.

On the other hand, here was Abbie. Dear, sweet, small-town-girl Abbie, who was so genuine you could smell it on her like a fragrance. Her parents ran a dairy farm in the same county as Lovett College. They made their own cheeses as a very successful side business, but it was hard work. They had three sons and a daughter and each of them did an equal share of the chores. The only dispensation from the farm was during track season, and after practices and meets, Abbie had to get her share done. Even if she had been interested in dating, the reality was, how in the blazes was she going to fit it in?

As luck would have it, the subject never came up. Abbie and Kyle were very similar in this area, to a point. But, where Kyle had very limited social experience, Abbie was the opposite. The Sanducci farm was along a main highway just outside of town, and since they sold milk and cheese, and their products were very, very good, there was a constant flow of customers. Abbie learned from her parents and older brothers the art of making small talk which translated into putting a person at ease so they felt comfortable around you. It also helped that Abbie inherited being a "people person" from both her parents who loved to have friends and family over.

So here Kyle stood, slowly wiping the excess water off his chin. There sat Abbie with a silly, beautiful grin on her face, staring right at him. There couldn't have been a more wide open invitation. Then came the announcement over the p.a. system: "Attention please. The library will be closing in fifteen minutes."

"Attention please, we've got a brain that is about to explode from over-stimulation! Stand back folks, it's going to be a real corker!" Abbie laughed.

"Corker?"

"Yeah, as in pop-goes-the-weasel!"

This time Kyle got it. In fact, he got it so well, that as he began to laugh he tripped where some of the water from the fountain had hit the floor and fell on his behind.

"Hey are you ok?"

"Yes. Yeah. I meant to do that."

"Of course."

"This sounds like bragging, but you should know that I'm attending this school on an extreme tripping scholarship."

"No way!"

"It's so exclusive that absolutely no one knew about it, until now."

"Don't worry, your secret's safe from the folks back home. I'll never tell a soul." Abbie put a finger to her lips for emphasis and eyed a group of students who were beginning to leave. "Spies," she said under her breath so only Kyle could hear. "Academic spies. Little goodie two shoes, the whole lot of 'em. I say we risk our cover, blow this popcorn stand, and get us some more pizza."

Doing their best to control themselves Kyle and Abbie didn't burst out laughing until they had gathered up their books, put on their coats and were outside, walking down the library steps towards town.

Maybe it was all those fresh vegetables covered in a tomato sauce that would have made any Sicilian proud. Maybe it was the two liter bottle of cola they shared. Neither one of them was used to drinking soda, but they knew they had a long night of studying ahead of them. Maybe it was the time of year. Maybe it was the night air.

Over dinner, both of them set a personal-best for laughing during a 20 minute time period. Ordinarily, they would have lingered over their meal. In turned out, this was another thing that Abbie and Kyle had in common. Abbie's family truly saw each meal as an anchoring point in the day. It was an occasion to catch up, eat good food, enjoy each other's company and engage in good natured ribbing. Kyle's family also saw meal time as something sacred, but in a different sort of way. For the Hoffman's meals meant conversation, discussion, debating, thoroughly exploring whatever subject was on the table. There was an openness that invited intellectual curiosity.

But next day was the last day of finals, and duty called across the table as they finished up their pizza and salads.

Both of them realized, point blank, how much they enjoyed the other's company.

Abbie began this portion of their conversation as they walked across the campus commons: "Hold on a sec, would you?"

Kyle obliged. Abbie took out a scrap of paper from her purse, wrote something on it and handed it over.

"It's my phone number. I was going to give it to you yesterday, but I chickened out."

Kyle was caught a bit off-guard. After all, as these things go, this was a first. It was also a first for Abbie.

"This is the part where you say something affirming," she coaxed, giving a tug to her bright woolen hat that was having a hard time covering her amazing head of blonde hair.

"What are you doing for Christmas?" Kyle recovered nicely.

"We have a family tradition, we stay home, eat plenty of good food and tease each other into oblivion," she nudged Kyle's side for emphasis. "How about yourself?"

"We're still looking for the Messiah, so I usually invite myself over to someone's house who's found him."

"That would earn you about ten ribbing points around the dinner table," she said, right before bursting out laughing. "You should come over if you're staying in town."

He didn't need any further prodding: "I'd like that very much."

And I hate to be the one to mention this, but as Kyle leaned over and gave Abbie a kiss it began to snow.

The Pumpkin Log

Mary Beth was minding her own business, crossing the street heading from the Kalamazoo Public Library towards the Park Club, when she glanced down and happened to notice a post-it note. It was a bright, unusually balmy autumn day, so she had no problem reading what was written on it. "Canned Pumpkin, Nutmeg, Walnuts, Cream Cheese, Eggs, Flour."

Of course, she thought, being a practically minded young woman. The ingredients for a pumpkin log! But there was something else that followed that sparked her imagination even further. A phone number that started with a 212 area code. She was struck by the juxtaposition of ingredients with a long distance area code.

She crossed South Street and sat down in Bronson Park. She got to thinking: What if it's some rich, big city psycho who was at the Park Club last night, got drunk, snatched his wife's shopping list, wrote down the phone number and planted this as a lark? No, that didn't make sense; if he was that much of a psychotic, he never would have gotten in to the Park Club to begin with, and why would his wife be writing down the ingredients to pumpkin log at a high-class shindig? Those sorts of people had cooks who were paid plenty to worry about such things.

Then Mary Beth thought: What if some woman had gone to the library to look up the ingredients and wrote them down?

Of course, she was from New York City and was in Kalamazoo for the holidays, working on an enormous project for corporate headquarters that necessitated going local for a while. So, in a burst of sentimentality, she took a break from work to write down the pumpkin log recipe, which got her to thinking about her boyfriend Armond. Who, even though he was French, most likely was a real creep. After all, how come he never went to see her at her West Side apartment? So, she got to thinking, 'To heck with him. I'm going to take a chance and look up the number of Wesley,' who was an outstandingly supportive co-worker who had made it known, in general terms, that he was interested in having dinner some time.

Wesley was supportive because, unlike Armond, he hadn't grown up in Alsace-Lorraine. To be sure, he was from Northern Ireland; Derry to be specific. And his parents, being the progressive type, had tagged him with a distinct un-Irish name so that it would make it that much harder to pin down his religious upbringing. He knew very well the importance of maintaining a low profile; deliberately remaining unassuming, even if his accomplishments left something to brag about. To Wesley, whatever academic kudos he received while attending Trinity College were secondary to who he was. Which included being polite to a fault, quick to laugh and always realizing the importance of friendship.

But maybe the Park Club had nothing to do with the note at all? Maybe it was some poor schmuck who was on their way to the grocery store, after making a side trip downtown for some reason. They hurriedly stuck the note on top of their address book, meaning to transfer the phone number at some point. It was most likely, as simple as that.

Mary Beth sat down directly across from the fountain in the Park. She wasn't one to beat around the bush. She pulled out her cell phone and immediately punched in the number. But because she was also extremely practical, as soon as the phone on the other end began ringing, she hung up.

What am I doing? she asked herself. Do I really want to get myself involved in this? Maybe it's nothing, but then I have no idea of who might be on the other end of the phone. She sat up straight on the park bench because good posture lent itself to making good decisions. Thinking back a bit, she realized that the last time she'd been on an adventure was when she went into the People's Co-op and picked up a bottle of tahini salad dressing. "That's absolutely pathetic!" she whispered out loud as she hit the redial button.

The voice on the other line was feminine and quizzical. "Hello?"

"Hi!" Mary Beth paused to collect her thoughts before answering. Should she identify herself straight away to instill confidence on the other end? Or should she just begin with finding the post-it note? Better to at least explain who you are before getting into details she thought.

"I'm calling from Kalamazoo. My name's Mary Beth and I found something that I think is yours."

"You're in Kalamazoo and you found something of mine?" Amanda Hatfield was a trial lawyer and she specialized in class action suits. In the beginning it had actually been fun. She loved the feeling of hearing the judge pronounce "guilty" while slamming down the gavel and staring at the defendant. Of course the defendant was always the "bad guy." The corporation that had been charging too much, or the pharmaceutical company that hadn't quite done its homework, not to mention the banking folk who flat out lied to their clients, using shady business practices to line the pockets of their CEOs.

"Yes. A post-it note. With the ingredients for pumpkin log written on it."

Normally Amanda would have pounced on the evidence and brought the call to a quick conclusion. But the fact was, for some inexplicable reason, she decided to sidestep the obvious.

"So Mary Beth, how are things in Kalamazoo?"

"Pardon?"

"What's the weather like in your neck of the woods?"

Mary Beth couldn't help but laugh. It had been a long time since she had laughed so freely. Two years had passed since Marty had died, and she no longer winced when she mentioned his name in passing, but still, the hurt was there.

"It's actually a beautiful Midwestern autumn day here."

"That's great! I take it you're calling from outside? I can hear the traffic in the background."

"Yes. I'm sitting on a park bench downtown."

"Where is Kalamazoo anyway?"

"Michigan," she answered.

"Oh, the Great Lake State."

"Don't say that to a native. It's not going to get you on their good side."

"I take it you're a dyed-in-the-wool then?"

Mary Beth wasn't about to get into her heritage or family history. So she didn't mention that she was actually from Middlebury, just across the border in Indiana. A Michiana transplant. She hadn't really set foot in Michigan until she started attending Olivet College, and she had wound up choosing Olivet by accident.

Through high school she had worked part-time for the Middlebury paper, intent upon pursuing a journalism degree. There was a young, curly haired, just-graduated intern working as a reporter. For some reason, Mary Beth thought she overheard that the guy had gone to Olivet. So during her senior year, she applied there. Three years after graduation, she found out the intern had actually gone to Albion College, so the joke was on her. She particularly remembered Professor Hendrickson, who had taught a senior seminar on Chaucer's Canterbury Tales, instructing the class in Middle English on the side. To this day, Mary Beth was one of the few persons she knew who could recite the opening lines by heart:

"Whan that Aprille with its shoures soote

The droghte of March hath perced to the roote,

And bathed every veyne in switch licour,
Of which engendred is the flour..."

This remembrance had the effect of changing Mary Beth's mind about revealing personal history. "No, I'm not dyed-in-the-wool. I'm from Michiana," she freely admitted.

"Mich-a-wata?" It was Amanda's turn to let out a laugh.

"Northern Indiana. That section of the Indiana-Michigan border they call Michiana."

This woman is really offering me a ton of information, gratis, thought Amanda. Ironically, she seemed to have that effect on people, but she was pretty sure it was because of her line of work, not because of her personality. Truth be told, Amanda was as slow as a tortoise on vacation when it came to offering personal details. Like, she always slept on the left side of the bed. Since she was a little girl, when she had to make room for Roxie, her golden retriever. Amanda had hazel eyes, with blue specks in them that stood out when she was perturbed. In the court room, the prosecution almost always had the opportunity to see those bright blue specks. She could cook a mean pasta with meatballs, chalking it up to her Italian-Norwegian ancestry. In fact, growing up, her father had spoken only Italian in the house until he began grade school. And he had made it a point to teach her the correct way of making pasta sauce from scratch.

"Middlebury, huh? Sounds charming. Is it anything like Mayberry?"

Mary Beth found herself enjoying the conversation so far, so she continued. "Well, as far as I know Andy Griffith never came within 500 miles of my home town. But again, I can't say the same for Barney or Aunt Bee or Opie."

"And if they didn't take the time to visit, most likely that would rule out Gomer or Goober or Floyd the Barber too, right?"

Although Amanda was a big-city girl, she grew up watching reruns of "The Andy Griffith Show," and she had found herself attracted to the place. A small town where everyone seemed to be mostly in a good mood and took the time to chat with their neighbors. Where Amanda grew up, a neighborhood was your apartment building and you were lucky to know who lived across the hall from you. So your friends became the doorman, or the guy down the street who sold you the morning newspaper, or the owner of the coffee shop on the corner who you could count on to be there even though it seemed like there was a revolving door of wait-staff who came and went continually. Which was why she had bonded with Wesley, another lawyer in her office.

"So, what's with the pumpkin roll? You don't sound like the bake-it-from-scratch type." It wasn't like Mary Beth was a detective. She was picking up bits and pieces from what Amanda was telling her. And it sure wasn't cooking tips. Her feminine intuition was registering a successful but lonely woman on the other end of the line.

"My boyfriend Armond was getting the ingredients for me," Amanda began to explain. "He must have written down my cell phone number so he wouldn't forget it in case he had to double check the recipe."

"Your boyfriend came to Kalamazoo to pick up the ingredients?"

How romantic! Thought Mary Beth. Some guy gets on a plane and flies almost a thousand miles one-way to find the ingredients to bake his girlfriend a holiday dessert? Marty had been that way. He was the kind of guy who would constantly surprise you, catching subtle cues and following them to a marvelous, amazing conclusion. Like one time when the two of them were walking along the Burdick Street mall, she began to eye a ski jacket in Gazelle Sports' window. A week later, Marty had booked them a weekend at Timberlake Resort which they had enjoyed immensely.

Amanda continued, "He was trying to make up for standing me up on our birthday plans to visit his parents. We had booked the flight and made all the arrangements. But then, three weeks out he got cold feet and said it wasn't a good time for a visit because his parents were going through some difficulty."

"But that's totally understandable. Who wants to visit parents when they're arguing?"

"His parents don't argue. They've been married for 100 years and they're fine. It's Armond who needed space."

"But what was he doing in Kalamazoo?"

"He wasn't. The nearest he's been was Detroit."

Armond was a purchaser for Macy's and had been assigned to lend support for the Fall line to the Detroit flagship store. And when 34th Street made a decision, you accepted it gracefully. Even if you felt like corporate didn't know what they were doing. Funny how he didn't mention any side trip to Kalamazoo.

"But there's local service, at least a couple of flights out of Detroit Metro Airport, back and forth, each day," Mary Beth noted. "So, it's not like it would have been impossible for him to come here."

"Why on earth would he travel out of his way to get ingredients for pumpkin log? It doesn't make sense. It's not like him at all."

"It sounds like he was trying to be romantic."

"He could have googled 'pumpkin log' on the Internet for goodness sakes. He didn't have to go to Kalamazoo."

"But it's romantic. And he's French. That's what French people do."

What Amanda didn't know was that, through the culinary grapevine, he'd heard that the pastry chef at the Park Club made extraordinary pumpkin log. Mainly because he choose fresh ingredients. Like home-grown pumpkin and fresh cream by way of Plainwell's Ice Cream Company.

Armond was motivated to track all of this down because of a dream he'd had, involving Amanda floating away, up in the sky. The two of them had been standing on Cape Cod, watching the sunset. The water was unusually warm and they were standing close enough to the shore to feel the water as it lapped against their toes. They were looking into each other's eyes when, suddenly, Armond noticed Amanda's blue specks appearing. What in the world? he thought. He only had time enough to give Amanda a quizzical look before she began to float away. "I'm sorry! I'm so sorry!" she said, almost at a whisper. As she ascended over his head, she simply said, "Isn't this romantic?!" He could only watch, dumbfounded, as she rose out of sight. "Hey goofus!" he heard the voice coming from the beach below. He looked down to find a sea-gull peering directly at him. "This is what happens when you refuse to take the crosstown bus!"

In an instant Armond had realized how selfish he'd been. Living in his East Side apartment, he hadn't given a thought about never coming to her place on West 89th Street. Amanda's apartment was smaller. But he'd figured between the two of them, she had the money to take a taxi. Besides, she didn't really have the time to cook, which he loved to do, and she didn't have much of a kitchen. He had figured his culinary skills were the perfect expression of his feelings. But obviously something had gotten lost in the translation.

"Mary Beth, I like pumpkin as much as the other person, but I think it's a question of intention. Maybe Armond did take a side-trip to Kalamazoo to pick up a recipe straight from the cook. But the point is, did he even bother to get to know me enough to know if I'd see that as a significant gesture?"

Wow thought Mary Beth. This woman sure is playing hardball! She thought back on the evenings that Marty and she had spent over kitchen masterpieces like substituting navy beans in the beans and franks dish, or how about tossing on some grated Kerrygold Dubliner on the cheese pizza? And the wine they drank came from Tiffany's Plaza, not some blown up pretentious place that made you pay to the gills for their knowledge of what was a good year or the advantages of South African over Spanish.

"So, if Armond's such a loser, who else might be on deck?"

"Well, there is this guy, in the office, actually."

This was getting interesting thought Mary Beth. Even if her own love life was on hold, she found Amanda's situation was perking her up.

"His name is Wesley. We've worked for the same firm for three years. In all that time, he's been nothing but supportive, encouraging me to go deeper in deposition work. That led to trail experience, which I love. And he's from Ireland. Northern Ireland, Derry."

How exotic to attract people from other countries, thought Mary Beth. West of Manhattan, outside of bigger cities, you didn't get that cosmopolitan influence. But was that really it? Did it all boil down to choices? Marty had been from Parchment. She grew up an hour away from him. And they met at Olivet College. Both from the same freshman class, meeting in the cafeteria within a few weeks of the start of fall semester. She hadn't been looking for anyone, concentrating on her studies. Which explains why she had been balancing a load of books on her tray when all of a sudden Dickens upset the apple cart, spilling everything on the floor. Marty had quickly moved from his spot in line to lend a hand.

"Let's get you another tray," he had said matter-of-factly. "How does a picnic on the grass outside sound?"

She had been so very grateful and amazed at the way he had turned such a disaster into an adventure. Mary Beth had readily accepted, and the rest, as they say, was history. So maybe this whole phone conversation was kismet. Was Mary Beth supposed to remind Amanda that all guys, at some point, were oblivious? That in the end it didn't matter because there was no such thing as the perfect person? Or was she supposed to encourage Amanda to go after Wesley? The guy seemed to be a peach. He probably had a killer brogue and thick wavy hair and sky blue eyes and a genuine sense of humor that was tempered with a kind nature. What girl wouldn't go head-over-heels for a guy like that? But Mary Beth couldn't get over Armond's gesture of coming to Kalamazoo. For all she knew, Armond had gone into the public library, just like she had, and walked across the very same intersection, and sat down on the very same park bench she was now using to chat with his girlfriend.

Mary Beth took a deep breath before responding. "So, tell me about the last time that you needed someone's forgiveness," she said.

"Pardon?"

"Can you tell me the last time you needed someone to forgive you?"

"What kind of a question is that?"

"I'm not sure, but do you mind answering it?"

There was something in Mary Beth's voice that told Amanda that she could trust her. Even if the question didn't seem to flow with the rest of the conversation. Something specific quickly came to mind.

"Actually, it was my neighbor down the hall. It was two weeks ago and it was pouring down rain. I was coming back from the grocery store and my arms were full. I barely was able to pull out my key to the front door and as I opened it, I heard my neighbor yell out, 'Could you please hold the door for me?' She was still on the main sidewalk down the street. I was struggling with the weight of the door against me. I could have just stuck my foot out to hold it for her, but I didn't. I figured, we crossed paths coming in and out of the building for at least three years. In all that time, I never asked her name. She never asked mine. I just knew we both lived in the same building, but that was it. We never held the door for each other before. I don't know why. I guess it could have been a sort of unspoken code. Don't offer to do that because it invites a conversation and I just didn't have time for that. Anyway, when I heard the door slam behind me, I felt awful. Part of me wanted to put down the grocery bags, find her and apologize on the spot. But I didn't. We haven't seen each other since, but for some reason I still feel like I need to ask her forgiveness for being rude. It's such a small thing. Silly, isn't it?"

"It doesn't sound like you think it's silly."

"Yeah, I've thought about it a lot and it strikes me at how this is such an ordinary event, but so important."

"An opportunity to extend some grace?"

"Right."

"Like Armond seems to be doing?"

In that moment, Amanda recognized Armond's actions for what they truly were. And she recognized the wisdom behind Mary Beth's question about forgiveness. She also realized that she was going to give Armond a second chance. Whether he deserved it or not wasn't the point. Amanda realized something else. In the course of a five minute phone conversation she had become friends with Mary Beth. She appreciated someone who could listen and tell her the truth.

"So, when was the last time you were in the Big Apple?" she asked.

"I've never been."

"I would love to invite you," said Amanda, "I make a mean spaghetti and meatballs and there's a guy named Wesley whom I'd like you to meet."

The Insomniac

Andy had grown really tired of the Big Apple.

He had spent eight years of his life there, which included getting a master's degree from Hunter College and working as the chief researcher for the National Coalition for the Homeless.

The director of the Jesuit's Volunteer Program at St. Francis of Loyola Parish had turned out to be a real horse's posterior. During Andy's interview he sat across from him, holding on to his walnut desk as if he were waiting to be transported to the Vatican at any moment.

No matter. He was sent on a wild goose chase to a food bank in Newark that needed someone to help out in the warehouse, sorting through grassroots food collections. As soon as he walked from the side entrance to the volunteer director's office, Andy realized that it wasn't his cup of tea. Yes, getting food to people was important, but the building was just a little too removed from the front lines. And after three years of doing nothing but research he was feeling the urge to have his statistical analysis verified by a little hands-on experience.

So he called up his friend Trevor at Joseph House, a Catholic Worker House of Hospitality back in Manhattan.

"Do you have an opening there?"

Trevor had laughed hysterically at the way that Andy had phrased it. "We aren't running a hotel, you know!" he said of the social outreach home that sat a stone's throw away from The Bowery. The basic gist of it was that Catholic Workers were on the front lines, serving and living with the poorest of the poor in the City. Dorothy Day and Peter Maurin had started the organization in the middle of the Great Depression and there remained a staunch commitment to "build a new society within the shell of the old."

In mid-July, Andy sublet his apartment in Inwood, packed up his clothes and books and, using a van borrowed from his former workplace, headed the 210 blocks down Broadway past 14th Street into Lower Manhattan. He had never driven in the City before, but he found the experience to be nothing short of exhilarating.

He had been at Joseph House only twice. One time had been to drop off some leftover chicken he had made for a party that didn't materialize. (Tim, who had been working the door that afternoon, was extremely gracious, considering that there wasn't enough food to feed more than half a dozen people, and at least 20 people lived at Joseph House.)

The other time he had come for a visit was when he was working on the Coalition's newsletter. Andy wanted to get graphic design advice from the editor of the Catholic Worker's newspaper, which was topnotch, featuring woodcuts from some of the more famous artists of the Catholic persuasion.

After Andy unloaded the van and brought it back to a parking lot uptown, he came back to join the live-in staff at Joseph House. The first person who met him in the kitchen that morning was Jeanne, from Ireland.

"Your reputation precedes you," she smiled, pouring herself a cup of tea.

"What reputation?"

"Word travels fast around the Worker, and there's a rumor that you're a grand one for suing the City and helping the homeless."

"I think you must have me mixed up with someone else."

(In fact, it was the Coalition's director, who was a lawyer, who did the litigating. Andy's place was researching the extent of homelessness in other cities.)

Jeanne raised her eyebrows mischievously. "Do I now? Are you going to sit there across the table from me and call me a liar?"

Good night, thought Andy. I'm ten minutes into the day, and I'm already upsetting the regulars.

"I'm sorry. It's just that I wasn't the one who spent time in the court room. I was a researcher, that's all."

"Rest easy, Mr. Andy," she said, her bright blue eyes giving her away. "I was only leading you on a wee bit. Actually I've been assigned to help show you the ropes, so to speak. There'd be no other reason that I would be on my two feet at this time in the morning. Unless I had house duty."

Jeanne explained that being "on the house" was split between two shifts. The first one began at six, with the responsibility of making coffee, tea and then setting out the cereal. As soon as that was done, six 15-gallon pots were put on the huge stove and half filled with water. Then, on an alternate day-by-day basis, they were filled with lentils, tomatoes or bullion and whatever other vegetables could be found in the cooler in the basement.

The first shift ended after the soup kitchen fed about 400 people, mostly from the Bowery area. After clean up, the second shift began, with the responsibility of answering the door and the phone, washing down the kitchen and setting up for supper. This was followed by cooking and serving the evening meal to about 20 people who lived at Joseph House (which was run as a home for men) and 25 other residents of Mary House (which was for homeless women).

After breakfast, Jeanne took Andy by the hand, leading him to the front door. "I'm not on house today, and neither are you, so we have the day pretty much to ourselves. That doesn't happen very often, so I suggest that you follow me out of here."

She was wearing a red flannel shirt and blue jeans, and was

five feet even, with a massive head of curly, jet black hair. "I'm a twin," she said. "Wouldn't you know that I got all the good looks and so my sister hardly speaks to me!"

"Really? That must be tough."

"Mr. Andy, you have to learn how to tell when a girl's leading you on. How have you ever survived this long? Or do I perceive that you don't have a girlfriend at the minute?"

"No, I don't." It wasn't exactly a sore point with him. Just a statement of fact. A fact that had caused much consternation living in a city of endless possibilities but no actuals. Andy was a transplanted Midwesterner, which hadn't helped. From day one in the Big Apple he had adjusted fairly quickly, except that the move from his home town hadn't helped his lack of experience with the opposite sex.

"Well, Mr. Andy, Not to brag, but I have had several romances. They were for the most part, very disappointing. Irish men are dunderheads when it comes right down to it. They aren't looking for a woman as much as they're looking for a mother. My sister Effie and I used to sing at the pubs in Dublin. There wasn't any work for us in our village and neither of us could afford university. So we made a fair living singing, saving our money up. Until I just got tired of the Irish boys trying to get me to do their laundry."

"So, you're a singer then?"

"Really, Mr. Andy, I've only given you half the story and there you go jumping to conclusions." They were walking across First Avenue now, on their way to NYU and the student union near Washington Square. "My sister and I decided to cut the cord. She stayed in Dublin and enrolled in Trinity College with a scholarship, while I came across the sea a year ago."

"But how did you wind up at the Worker? I mean, you don't strike me as being the social worker type."

(Neither was Andy, but he knew his time at Joseph House would be limited. As far as he was concerned, he was in-between jobs as he took time to sort things out before leaving the City for good.)

"I gave them a call. I had read their newspaper and loved the mission of living with the poor while serving them. It really intrigued me. And I have to admit, I think your country is grand."

Now it was Andy's turn to be astonished. "You mean the United States?"

"Of America!" she answered. "I love the freedom here. I love the bigness of this city and the bigness of this country and the possibilities. Besides, everyone from Ireland is in love with you."

"Is that so?"

"'Give me your tired, your poor, your huddled masses, yearning to be free!' America helped us out during the Potato Famine and we've never forgotten you for it. That's an Irishman's curse, I guess."

"A curse?"

"Yes, to have reality so colored by the past, due to sentimentality. It's not a very logical way to live."

Jeanne paused a moment to jump up on a brownstone's steps, so she was, for the moment, a good three inches taller than Andy, who was also on the short side. "This is a great smoochin' step," she observed, giving Andy the once over.

"A smoochin' step?"

"Yes. It's got the advantage of offering the ability to smooch eye-to-eye with your partner if you're a short person, like us."

At this observation Andy found himself turning red.

"Mr. Andy, did I embarrass you? I truly didn't mean to. I'm only making an observation, not a suggestion, at this point." She smiled directly at him.

What is the problem with this person, he thought. I don't even know her for heaven's sake, but she seems determined to ask herself out on a date.

"No, I mean, I wasn't taking it personally."

He didn't believe it was possible, but he felt himself turning a darker shade of red. He couldn't remember the last time a girl had embarrassed him. In fact it was in fifth grade when he was a Safety Patrol Boy and Betty Alario had told him, flat out, that she was in love with him before smacking his face in retaliation for being ignored.

"That's good, because I wouldn't want to embarrass you or have you take anything in a personal way, especially so soon after we've met. So, I've done a fair amount of the blabbering this morning. Why don't you tell me all about yourself?"

By this time Jeanne and Andy were walking inside the NYU Student Union. She motioned for them to sit down.

"The first thing is, I'm not a native New Yorker."

"Go on with 'ya."

"Actually, I've gotten to the point where I'm not exactly a fan of the City."

"Why is that?"

"It's a long story."

"I love stories!"

So Andy began to tell Jeanne how he had come to New York with some manuscripts in the hope of getting published. In the space of three weeks, he had gone to every publishing house in Manhattan and was dangerously close to running out of what money he had saved up. Reality set it and he got a job in a hospital nursing office. The pay was actually good, but the job sidetracked him, until he decided to go back to school to pick up an additional degree. Which eventually led him to an internship with a national advocacy group for the homeless. Idealism had gotten the better of him. It had been a great cause, but after three years of researching the subject, he was ready to do something hands on. But the Catholic Worker was just a stepping stone on the way home.

After listening intently, Jeanne skipped to the chase. "And after eight years, you haven't given your heart to anyone?"

"Not really."

"Well, shame on the women of these five boroughs for not recognizing a gem among the stones."

"How about you?"

"Haven't had time to snoop around the island yet. Although I've caught the eye of a few visitors at Joseph House. You could say I'm single and fancy free."

"Do you miss your home?"

"Oh aye! Every time it rains. The rain in Manhattan is an inconvenience. Where I come from, it's an invitation to a conversation. People are extraordinarily interesting, don't you think?"

"If you're an extravert. But for those of us who aren't of that persuasion, it can be difficult to deal with others."

Jeanne reached over and ruffled up his hair a bit before speaking. "If that's truly where you stand on the matter, then God's certainly got quite the sense of humor."

Andy found Jeanne's spontaneity appealing, even though it caught him off guard. "How's that?"

"You have landed at the world headquarters of a movement, and it attracts visitors from all over God's green acres. And they are going to come right up to you and ask a hundred questions and they won't leave you alone until you satisfy their curiosity. Not to mention the dear people of the street who will start talking with you whether you're in the mood or not. Then there's the rest of us who are working with you. Be that as it may, because you're an introvert, I may just tell you my secret hiding place, even at the risk of losing it for my own personal use."

His curiosity was definitely getting the better of him. He knew how difficult it was to find a truly quiet place in the City and once found, how reluctant the finders were to share it.

Two weeks later Andy was having trouble getting to sleep. It was past ten in the evening and it had been one of those days when the heat of summer was reflected off the city's concrete like a gigantic outdoor grill. He quietly got out of the men's dormitory on the third floor, walked two flights up and got on the roof. There was a slight breeze, enough to cause some relief, along with two lawn chairs. He sat down, closed his eyes and was almost asleep when he heard noise coming from the fire escape.

There was not much he could do to defend himself, but he found an empty clay pot, figuring that he might have a chance to hit the intruder over the head. Poised near the edge of the roof, he waited, pot above his head, ready to strike.

But as the person on the fire escape got closer to the top, they began to sing. It was a woman's voice and it was absolutely stunning in its clear, rich tone. In fact, the song had the effect of totally disarming Andy as he gradually put the pot back down. A few seconds later, Jeanne appeared, climbing off the escape.

"Why, Mr. Andy, I was going to tell you all about my secret place, but you had to go and spoil it!" she teased.

"How did you even get up here from the outside?"

"The gate to the backyard can't be secured. There's a lock on the chain and all, but everyone at the Worker knows it's a fake, meant to deter but nothing else."

Andy smiled as he sat back down on the chair, beckoning Jeanne to do likewise.

She sighed before continuing. "Isn't this the most delicious spot! This is where I tell God all my secrets."

"Your confessional?"

"Not my sins, my secrets. There's a huge difference you know." She once again eyed him thoroughly. "I'll tell you one of mine and then you tell one of yours. No one else will know, so they'll still be secrets to everyone else."

The relief from the heat and Jeanne's song had worked some sort of magic on Andy. He nodded as he took a deep breath of her fragrance, now so extremely close.

"I may be an extrovert, but I'm like you at the same time."

"What do you mean?"

"Even extroverts feel the need to get away from it all. But that's not my secret. That's more like an observation. Sort of a tidbit thrown in for free so that you'd appreciate the secret itself that I'm about to tell you."

"Got it."

"Mr. Andy, your first morning here, for some unexplainable reason, from the moment that you walked into the kitchen, I began to like you. I mean, seriously, I could hardly take my eyes off of you." Jeanne paused for a moment and took a deep breath. "How's the secret going so far?"

"You've got me hooked."

"Well, actually, it started when your friend Trevor showed me a picture of you. It was a snapshot of a group at the beach. I immediately cued in on you and asked him who you were. When he told me that you were going to be coming to Joseph House, my heart did a flip-flop. Sort of ridiculous, isn't it?"

"You mean love before first sight?"

"No, this was deeper. More significant. It was like destiny." (Jeanne realized just how much she was revealing to Andy, and it made her uncharacteristically shy. Normally, she had no qualms about expressing herself, but this was deeply personal.)

Andy was struck speechless. This sort of thing had never happened to him. Although the writer in him was definitely fueled by a sense of the romantic, he was mostly a logical person.

This has turned embarrassingly awkward, thought Jeanne. She too had never had this sort of talk with any man because she had never felt so deeply towards any of her boyfriends. "It's your turn," she said, staring straight ahead.

Andy reached out and gently moved Jeanne's hair away from her forehead. "I don't like pepperoni pizza."

She turned to him, punching him hard in the arm. "What kind of a silly-arsed secret is that? This isn't fourth grade, you know! I'm not letting you off this roof until you come up with something a lot better than that!"

"Hey, you pack quite a punch with those guns of yours!"

"Well, there's plenty more of where that came from, and I mean it! You better be prepared to come clean with a whopper of a secret or else you will come face to face with the famed Irish temper. Not to mention that you're about to incur the wrath of the firstborn!" (Jeanne's shyness had vanished and she was back to being her old self, thank God.)

"Wrath of the first born?" (Andy came from a big family, five siblings in all, but he had never thought about birth order, although he was right in the middle.)

"We first-borns are very independent and tend to fight for our way so you better fess up quick!"

"That first morning when you walked into the kitchen, I noticed how beautiful you were. And as you took me for our walk I began to sense how smart and funny you were. In fact, you are far and away the most disarming woman I have met in this City, or anyplace else."

Jeanne smiled broadly. "Tell me more."

"That's one secret right there, isn't it?"

"I told you a load of them." She edged closer. "I suggest you keep going."

"When you showed me the smoochin' stoop I wanted to test it out on you right then and there."

"So why didn't you?" Oh these American men, she thought. Acting so super-masculine but when it came right down to it, they were all talk and no action, especially when it came to expressing their feelings.

"Because timing is everything. And it's much more romantic to kiss someone under the evening sky, when the bustle of the City isn't getting in the way of the experience."

Andy put his arm around Jeanne. And as he kissed her and she wrapped her arms around him, he could identify Jeanne's fragrance. It was lavender and cocoa butter.

Patience

Sure, patience is a virtue. But for Lissie Simon, it was getting to be downright ridiculous.

She was 37 and had wanted a baby (lots of them, actually) and a husband, ever since she could remember. In fact, in first grade, Lissie got sent to the Principal's Office for bringing her baby doll to class. Fast forward to junior high and she was still at it. This time, she got caught with back issues of Bride Magazine in her locker. Boy, did she catch holy-heck for that. And don't get me started about high school.

It was senior year. Mid-April. Just after spring break and everyone was focused on the prom. It was all anyone was talking about. In the halls. In the locker rooms. In the stairwells. In the cafeteria. Everywhere. The whole school had prom-on-the-brain. Including Lissie. Why would she be immune? She was all of five-feet, four-inches and holding, with bright red hair, the color of fresh carrots, and hazel eyes to die for.

Lissie was having a difficult time lining up a date for the prom because of an inexplicable drive to tell the truth. No matter what. And the 'what' in this case turned out to be going through high school dateless. But she solved her dilemma by going with Stefan Olsen, the school janitor.

Stefan was 65 years of age and from the old country. He was proud of the fact that he was Swedish. His Dad was from Stockholm and his Mom from Russia. Although he didn't attend church, he nonetheless was very spiritually-minded. Stefan had a thick head of snow-white hair and was a very good dancer. He also looked a lot like Michael Douglas, which didn't hurt. And he had a definite sense of humor and was great at making small talk, which helped immensely when Stefan knocked on Lissie's door and had to explain to her parents why a senior citizen Swede was taking their daughter out.

Besides her physical attractiveness, Lissie was a brain. Her most favorite topic happened to be Einstein's theory of relativity, although she had no intention of pursuing it academically. She had a poster of Einstein framed on her bedroom wall, right across from her bed so she saw it first thing when she got up every morning. It was the one with him riding a bicycle. A reminder that you could like quantum physics and still keep your sense of humor. She was known to start her day by sitting up, smiling and saying (out loud): "Good morning Albert! Let's make it a great day!"

She also liked Gregorian chants, and was a huge fan of Hildegard von Bingen.

It was during her senior year that Lissie and her brother began to conduct what they loosely termed "ESP experiments." Where, spontaneously, they would look at each other, one would say, "the first three numbers that come to mind, now!" Or "the first three colors." Or "the first three cities." And they would speak them out. More often than not, their similitude was 100%. Every time that happened they would stare at each other for a split second and then burst into peals of laughter. When they became adults, they got into the habit of calling each other at 9 p.m. every Wednesday. Asking each other: "What are you thinking about, right now?" And when they would compare notes, practically always they would be thinking of the same subject.

While you might expect the opposite, this unusual closeness with her brother only fed Lissie's desire to settle down. Her preference was for a family of six kids, living on a dairy farm. Her husband would be a full-time farmer, while she ran a graphics design business from home.

All of this was well and good, but, unfortunately Lissie lived in Ann Arbor, Michigan. She was a tenured professor and she had a home within walking distance of Geddes Arboretum, which was nowhere near any kind of a farm.

She loved Zingerman's, not only because of the food, but because all of the staff had these wonderfully sincere smiles – like the crews at McDonald's used to have. And when they asked, "Is there anything else I can get you?" you truly wished there were because they meant it.

As luck would have it, Lissie's one desire, besides having six kids, 20 Holsteins and a husband was to travel to New Zealand. She kept a passport handy, carrying it in her purse at all times, "just in case." At the moment it was unstamped, but she was romantically minded enough to one day envision herself giving in to dreams of lush green meadows filled with contented sheep, lazily gazing away under the southern hemisphere's sunshine.

She didn't know beans about New Zealand really, but, outside of the classroom, she wasn't the type to complicate her dream life by actively pursuing it.

"When the time comes, I'll know it," she told her best friend, Borden Smyth, who happened to be a staff writer for the Ann Arbor Observer "There's an unmistakable universal order of things that you just can't get in the way of."

"Explain yourself!" said Borden, shutting off her laptop right before the battery went dead. Even though Smyth grew up in Boulder during the 70's, the closer she got to retirement, the more conservative she had gotten in her thinking. To the point that going for a stroll along Main Street made her nervous.

Lissie shook her head: "It requires faith and you can't quantify it."

"Oh, poppycock, Lissie! Stop talking like an English major."

"But I am an English major," retorted Lissie. "I know what I'm talking about."

"You can't build a case against the law of inertia. Sit still and you'll remain at rest."

"That's motion. I'm talking about real life."

"So am I, Lissie!"

"If you won't believe me, will you believe Newton?"

"What about him?"

"Why do you think he was under the apple tree in the first place? Just sitting around, waiting to discover gravity?"

"Basically."

"How about the possibility that he was sitting there because he had his heart broken and he didn't know what to do."

"Newton was a scientist."

"Sure, but he was also a human being."

"And your point is..."

"My point is that Isaac Newton's reason for being under the apple tree was to stave off depression, by communing with nature. He had absolutely no intention of discovering anything."

Borden only raised her eyebrows and leaned back. She knew better than to continue a line of argument that Lissie wasn't even half-way interested in pursuing.

"I'm going out to grab a bite. What to come?"

"No thanks. I have a student coming in ten."

But Lissie really didn't have a student coming in ten. She wasn't hungry because cognitive dissonance killed her appetite. She hadn't had a decent meal in a week and had been pretty much subsisting on Orville Redenbacher's version of popcorn.

Popcorn was her go-to comfort food. As those things go, it wasn't all that bad. It filled you up and provided roughage, so at least you kept things clean and flowing while life was serving up curveballs.

She went home, picked up her Bible and opened it up spontaneously to the Book of Esther, the seventh chapter, where Haman gets himself hanged after plotting to kill the Jews. It started out as a wine banquet with Haman being invited to join King Xerxes and Esther, but things wound up pretty badly for Haman. The poor guy was so nervous that he literally fell all over Esther trying to explain his order to have all the Jews killed. He succeeded only in ticking off the King, so Haman was hanged on the very gallows he had built for Mordecai (Esther's uncle whom Haman detested).

The interesting thing about all this is that Esther probably wasn't going to tell King Xerxes who had ordered all the Jews killed until he asked her who dared to be so presumptuous to do such a thing. She could have given Haman the tenth degree in front of the King at any time, but she held off.

What amazing patience, thought Lissie. I could use more of that! Which led her to think: I wonder if patience is linked somehow with judgment. It seems to me if a person is patient, then, for openers, they'd be less inclined to rush into a rash observation. All I have to do is catch a sideways glimpse of someone and I have them all pegged. Peripherally induced prejudice is horribly short-sighted.

It reminded Lissie of the time in college when she was stricken with a guy wearing horn-rimmed glasses who was a French major. She had seen him every day during that first week of the semester and had made up her mind to say hello. One fateful day as she found herself standing next to him in the cafeteria line, she summoned up the courage.

"So, you must have the meal plan, huh?"

"Yes."

"I noticed that you don't pick up the meat entrees."

"Right."

"Are you a vegetarian?"

"No, I just don't like eating meat."

So far, so good, thought Lissie. He's not a vegetarian, he's willing to converse. Let's keep going.

"Any particular reason why?"

"I grew up on a farm. My dad raised beef and I got tired of eating it."

"But there's other types of meat besides beef."

"They all have the same taste to me. I learned to get my protein from other sources."

O.K, thought Lissie, this is going nowhere, especially if I'm in the market for a dairy farmer. Leave the meat thing alone for now and move on.

"Have you declared a major yet?"

"French. I'm going to teach it. High school level."

It was at that instant Lissie noticed that the boy had a nervous habit of flaring his nostrils. And when he flared them they became something like five times bigger than normal. It was actually sort of disgusting, but that wasn't the judgment that she placed on him. Lissie's judgment was linked to the fact that he didn't ask her any questions in return as they were getting their meal. What was the problem with a guy who couldn't respond to a casual conversation by being a little interested in its forward movement? So, after that incident, Lissie never gave the French major with the horn-rimmed glasses much thought. Which was a shame, because he had wanted to ask her to join him for lunch that day but was just as socially awkward as she was.

Fast forward to Friday after Lissie taught her last class for the day. It was an afternoon class on Dickinson. Paul was a good 15 years older than anyone else in the room, which made him about the same age as Lissie. He was a personal banker. And no matter where the classroom discussion led, he always seemed to hold back.

"Typical banker," thought Lissie. "So uptight and impersonal; if you can't sum it up on a spreadsheet for him, forget about it."

She was walking down the hallway towards the side door which led to the staff parking lot, looking forward to the weekend because she hadn't assigned any homework. Thoughts of a nice warm bath, a glass of red wine and a good book to read brought a smile to her face. Ever so slowly, her mind began to upwind, just like gentle waves hypnotically lapping at the shoreline. Until Paul's voice interrupted.

"Miss Simon?"

Lissie reluctantly turned around to face him. "Yes?"

"I know you're not on the clock, so to speak, but do you mind if I ask a question?"

Strike one, thought Lissie. Don't ask me if you can ask a question. Just go for it!

"Shoot."

"Well, I was wondering about a couple of Dickinson's poems 'There is a word,' and 'One Crucifixion.' I mean, do you suppose there's a connection to them?"

Of course there is, thought Lissie. Strike two. Every poem that a poet creates is somehow connected to others they've penned. Why would it be any different with Emily Dickinson?

"It's possible."

"Why would she write the lines: 'Our Lord – indeed – made compound witness – And yet – there's newer – nearer Crucifixion than that.' And four years earlier she wrote: 'Behold the keenest marksman! The most accomplished shot! Time's sublimest target Is a soul forgot!'"

Good heavens, thought Lissie. Does Dickinson have to balance her checkbook for you? Strike three!

"But don't you think it's interesting?"

"What's interesting?"

"That Dickinson wrote about the Crucifixion four years before she wrote about the soul forgot!"

"Why would that matter?"

"Because you'd think as a person gets older, the possibility of being forgotten would become sharper and much more painful. But, maybe that's why she's referring to the newer, nearer crucifixion."

All of a sudden, Lissie stopped judging because she was awestruck at what she saw in Paul's eyes. The man's brain had been working triple-overtime, putting concepts together, and he was just now gaining understanding. This was one of Lissie's all-time favorite moments as an instructor. She loved lecturing and all the preparation that went with it, but she absolutely lived for the discussion that followed.

So, she thought. Paul's not some stuck-up banker who comes to class in three piece suits to impress everyone else. This guy is genuinely interested in experiencing beauty. As far as Lissie was concerned, he had just hit a home run.

(Point of fact: Paul wore three piece suits to class because he didn't have time to change into anything else before heading for campus. He didn't have time for dinner either. Of course Lissie hadn't eaten yet, but he didn't know that.)

Lissie was still thinking about what Paul had said and was immensely enjoying the look in his eyes.

She stopped walking and sat down on a bench, inviting Paul to have a seat next to her. "Well, the thing about Dickinson was that she could be such an enigma. Deeply personal while extremely shy. Small town girl but incredibly sophisticated, very proper but amazingly adventurous."

"I think the key that links the two poems together is the line, 'One Calvary, exhibited to stranger, as many be, as persons, or peninsulas, Gethsemane, is but a province, in the being's centre.'"

"So, you're saying that loneliness was the key element of the Crucifixion?" questioned Lissie.

"I'm saying that it was Jesus' loneliness on the cross that killed him just as much as our sins."

How could this be coming out of the mouth of a banker? Lissie thought. She couldn't help herself. She took a deep breath before continuing on: "But you work for a bank, right?"

Paul threw his head back and laughed. "I admit bankers have done a lot of sinning, but I don't think all of us in the industry deserve to be crucified."

Lissie blushed. "No, I mean, how often do you think like this?"

Paul laughed again. "Pardon?"

Now it was Lissie's turn up at the plate and she was swinging at sliders. Strike one!

"I'm sorry," Lissie was desperately trying to cover her tracks. "It's just that I don't often encounter non-traditional students who are like you."

Paul was on the pitcher's mound now and he kept the sliders coming. Strike two. "So, what I do for a living determines who I am in your book?"

"No. Absolutely not. I'm afraid I'm giving you the wrong impression. I've been teaching here for twelve years. God knows I've come across some characters. My students continually surprise me, but..." Lissie stopped talking. She had the strangest feeling as if she were standing outside of herself, listening in to the conversation, and she didn't like what she was hearing.

She could feel her heart racing and she knew she'd been caught in a lie. She could either keep heaping it on, and then excuse herself, or 'fess up.

Summoning up all the courage inside her, Lissie looked Paul straight in the eye. "The fact of the matter is, I reach conclusions about people pretty quickly. Quite often those conclusions have no basis in reality. Here I am asking you how a banker could have legitimate opinions about Emily Dickinson. The funny thing is, most of the time I wouldn't really care to dissect it, and I certainly wouldn't go out of my way to confess intellectual snobbery to a student."

Luckily for Lissie, Paul's line of work had taught him to be extremely open-minded. Every day he had to sit across the desk with people who were letting him in to one of the most intimate aspects of their life. Most Americans wouldn't blush in telling you any other personal tidbit, but bring up the subject of their wealth, and it was a totally different story. Going to a financial counselor was ten times worse than going to confession. So he had developed a keen sixth sense about character, and he could see beyond her admission to the courage that caused Lissie to speak it out. He knew he could rear back and toss another slider, or patiently walk off the pitcher's mound altogether.

"I don't like canned green beans," he said.

"What?"

"I just don't like canned vegetables. Especially green beans."

"Oh."

"Want to know something else?"

"OK.

"I don't like microwave popcorn either."

"Really?"

"I have an old-fashioned popcorn maker that uses real butter."

Lissie was impressed. "Wow!"

"And I could kill for some Thai food right now."

"I'm actually starving. Could we continue this conversation over dinner?"

So there on the outskirts of academia, a student and teacher inconspicuously got up and walked into what was becoming a beautiful evening.

Lunch Among the Aliens

Mac worked in a factory that employed a thousand workers. The vast majority of them were in pharmaceutical production. In an effort to promote better communication, they were broken up into teams, like the Roman army had legions of a hundred. That way, if there was contamination at any point along the process, the damage could quickly be contained.

There was one cafeteria on the campus that fed all of the workers. Each shift took their meal break in 15 minute staggered starts. Which meant that normally each group of ten workers within a legion wound up sitting next to each other. In theory it was meant to encourage camaraderie as well as foster efficiency. The reality was that on this particular Tuesday at 11:15 a.m., Mac was feeling bored by the lack of much of a social life fed by co-workers.

It wasn't that he was anti-social as much as he was shy. In grade school he had been saved by the familiarity of neighborhood kids attending the same school and the natural flow from the school day into everyday life. Experiences were shared and friendships were deepened on the walks to and from school. But from middle school on, as soon as he was bused to the building, everything changed.

Mac had been born on the tail end of the baby-boomer generation, at a time when school buses were filled to the gills and being forced to sit with a bunch of strangers, on a gerrymandered route, wasn't his cup of tea. By the time he hit high school he was used to talking only when spoken to and never outside of the classroom.

His college experience had only reinforced Mac's lack of social skills outside of the immediate neighborhood.

So here he was, 17 years after graduation, making the maximum grade allowable as part of a team that produced some 12,000 pills a day. Which, on one level could have been seen as remarkable, but on the other hand, how much extra-strength pain reliever did the world need?

After filling up his tray with a vegetable stew that looked enticing, Mac found an empty table for two in the corner, and he decided to go for it, looking forward to a little peace and quiet for a change. He wasn't at the table five minutes before a co-worker walked up.

"Excuse me, but is this seat taken?" she asked.

He looked up at her before reluctantly answering, "No. Feel free."

"Thanks!" She sat down with an uncommon gracefulness. "I'm Melanie. I work in antihistamines, Building D."

"Mac. Team 34, right in this building."

She smiled as she picked up her fork to take a bite of salad. "So, how long have you been working here?"

"A long time. Started straight out of college."

"BS in chemistry?"

"Yes."

"I just started here, about a year ago. They hired me through a temp agency, but a permanent position came up and I grabbed it. Can't knock the benefits."

Actually, I could, thought Mac. But he didn't want to go there. Six years ago, management had started to chip away at the benefit package, and it had reached the point where new hires had no pension to speak of. In response, there had been some talk about inviting a union representative in to chat with the line workers. But the word at the water cooler was that the union rep. had been given a false impression and so had placed an outreach action as a low priority until there was a stronger measure of support.

"The management here overall is fair," said Mac, "but there are times when it could use a little prodding." And he had to remind himself that he was part of management now. He had started on as a line worker, advanced to section leader, then shift leader and now he was a project coordinator.

"So, are you a native of Kalamazoo?" she asked.

"Born and bred. Even went to Western Michigan University. How about you?"

"Bloomingdale."

Mac softly whistled. "Wow, towns don't come much smaller do they?"

Melanie laughed. "Our claim to fame is being the midway point on the Kal-Haven Trail. And being the birthplace of two famous Hollywood types like Betsy Palmer and David Wayne to boot."

"College?"

"Central Michigan University. I didn't want to live within commuting distance."

"The things we do for love, huh?"

At this point, Mac knew he was interested in Melanie, but he figured, what was the point? He was thinking that because their ID badges were color coded, she already knew that he was a manager. None of the line workers wanted to hang out with managers – it was an unwritten code of conduct. If you worked the line, you were taking orders from management all day long, so why would you deliberately choose to be with someone who was workroom groomed to continue to give orders after hours?

Then why was Melanie acting like she was interested in him? Was she trying to find out something about Mac through the back door? To use against him later? For goodness sake, this wasn't high school! She needed to get beyond management vs.

production and figure out that they were all on the same team. A good line saved money, and the company showed its appreciation by rewarding line workers that were part of a team that achieved.

If there was one thing that Mac had learned in his nearly two decades of corporate employment it was that at the end of the day, the bottom line was always something measurable and if you achieved it, nothing worked better than monetary reward to reinforce productive behavior. Who would have thought that his Introduction to Philosophy class would have come in handy on the factory floor? All that academic achievement put a polish to his sarcasm.

Melanie didn't quite get his remark about her college choice. "Pardon?"

"You said you went to Central Michigan because you didn't want to be within commuting distance. Sounds like there may not have been an excess of familial love to bind you to home?"

"Why would you think that?" Her smile was either ironic or an expression of openness. Which, Mac wasn't quite sure, but either way, it was outstandingly beautiful. "My family is actually very close. Two older brothers who were my all-time favorite protectors and encouragers, and a dad and mom who showed me how to live life without regrets."

"So why did you choose a college that was away from home?"

"I loved the school nickname."

"Chippewas?"

"Yes."

"Are you part Native American?"

Melanie laughed before answering. "No, are you part horse?" in reference to the Western Michigan University mascot being the Broncos.

For the first time in their conversation, Mac cracked an inkling of a smile. "Point taken. But the fact remains that you chose a school for a very non-traditional reason. Did you enjoy your time there?"

"I had an absolute blast. I read tons of books outside of

classroom assignments. And I met the most interesting people. One of my best friends has been a nanny in Austria for years."

"No kidding."

"Austrian families love her because she helps them to practice their English on the side. Another one of my friends from Central works for a tennis cable channel and she's travelling all over the world covering tournaments. She's in Japan as we speak."

Mac noticed that conversation seemed to flow from Melanie like water from a fountain.

"How about you?" he asked.

"Four siblings altogether. Two of each. Two of us live in Michigan, and two live out of state."

"What about your parents?"

"Both alive and well and totally in love with each other," she replied. "This year they celebrate their fortieth wedding anniversary."

Melanie adored her parents. They had raised their children in an atmosphere of freedom. They had a home a stone's throw away from the village, but their backyard faced a 10 acre stretch of woods. Because of this, and the fact that she was an only girl, Melanie pretty much grew up your classic tomboy. Summers were spent rambling around the woods, and tagging along with her brothers as they played endless games of baseball and kick-soccer in the backyard which included at least an acre of grass that was used as a neighborhood playground.

Because she spent a disproportionate amount of her summer in the company of boys, Melanie had never been flummoxed by them. In fact, because she had learned to speak her mind with her brothers' friends, she naturally spoke up in the company of the opposite sex. If anything, she found the less upfront ways of female communication to be a bit perplexing.

"So are you the older or younger brother?"

"Two years older, but I've got one older sister and one younger. She's a MD now. I'm the classic middle child of the lot."

Mac had been fiercely protective of his younger sister,

screening her would-be boyfriends. The ones that he didn't intimidate by the "I've got my eyes on you" look were quickly discouraged by his younger sister's wit and athletic ability. The truth was, she was more agile and talented than most boys her age, and she was academically at the top of her class. Mac had been proud of her back when she was a kid and continued to be proud of her all through medical school.

So he was familiar with the intricacies of sharing secrets. You had to earn the right to engage in that level of intimacy.

There comes a point in any cafeteria conversation where a mostly subconscious decision is made. How deep do I want to go during my lunch hour? For openers, by the time a person got from their workstation to their table, they were lucky to have 40 minutes left, if you considered the fact that most often, you were expected to be back on the job within an hour of leaving your station.

And most of the time you couldn't count on having a one-on-one. The tables weren't set up that way and form followed function to a "t." But even if Melanie and Mac had been sitting on a picnic table in the middle of nowhere, he still would have found himself fumbling due to being so out of practice.

Most afternoons after work, he looked forward to going home, doing some odds-and-ends chores around the house, and then putting his feet up as he soaked in the peace and quiet of the neighborhood. To him, the laughter of the kids on his block as they played outside was actually soothing in comparison to the methodical undercurrent of machinery. No matter how long a person worked in an industrial type of setting, you never quite got used to it. The first thing most production workers noticed as soon as they walked out the employee entrance was the peace caused by the relative lack of noise.

"Ever been married?" she asked.

The question came out of the blue and surprised him. It wasn't as if Mac was opposed to talking about it, but he wasn't the type to dig into subjects that had the potential for being painful. The fact was, he had been married once, but only for four years. And looking back on it, even though it had been over ten years ago, he was amazed at how two people could have lived together and shared a life, day in and day out, and yet hardly known each other.

"Yes, but it was only a few years and we really weren't that close." It felt odd to say it out loud.

"Not much in common?"

"More like being married was a role that we couldn't play very well. It didn't come natural to either of us."

Most of Melanie's friends were married. Even though she was relatively young - she'd turned 34 last September - she often felt out of place in the company of married couples.

"So you got tired of faking it?"

Mac smiled. "I guess you could say that. How about yourself?"

"When I was younger, I was having too much fun being single so marriage wasn't a big priority. A friend of mine once told me that if you wanted to be married, you should live like you want to be married, and I wasn't willing to do that."

"But your parents were a great example of two married people who seemed to actually enjoy each other. Why wouldn't that rub off on you?"

"Well, I sort of hit a rebellious phase I guess." This time it was Melanie's turn to laugh out loud. She caught herself, realizing where they were. "Oops!" She lowered her voice before continuing. "You said that your parents had been married for a long time, but you didn't say what their relationship was like."

"People don't always stay married because they love each other."

"Shocking, isn't it?"

"I have a habit of overstating the obvious." Mac smiled.

"It's not overstating. I appreciate your honesty. You have no idea how often people who are supposed to be friends sugar-coat the truth."

Melanie frowned. Why was she even mentioning that? It wasn't like she had made a ton of friends recently. Actually, she hadn't developed any substantial friendships since college. She had graduated, fully intending to keep in touch, and she did, with a few people. But it was mostly long distance, "this is what I've been up to lately, how about you," sort of thing. Enough to keep you updated without getting involved about it.

It wasn't that Melanie was opposed to friends, or that she was negative minded, because she wasn't. She was spontaneous and free and happy for the most part, but at this point in her life, she was perfectly fine with going to a concert by herself.

"Are we finding it a bit difficult to trip the light fantastic with a significant other then?" Mac asked.

"Who came up with that phrase, anyway?"

"Trip the light fantastic?"

Melanie shook her head. "'Significant other'. What's that supposed to mean? You're either married or not, right?"

"O.K." Mac wasn't sure where this was going, but he knew enough about human nature to give Melanie room to explain.

"I mean, it's not that I'm a prude or anything. That's not the point. Why not call a spade a spade? Instead of introducing someone as your significant other, why not say, I'd like you to meet Paxton; he's the guy I've been living with for five years but haven't gotten around to marrying yet."

"I guess that's one way of looking at it."

"Of course it is. And what happens if Paxton and I had a kid two years into being each other's significant other and he chooses to up and leave so he can be a significant other to someone else? Where does that leave me and my child?" Melanie felt herself starting to hyperventilate. "Hypothetically speaking."

"Right. It's all hypothetical. So, you're telling me that you have a child whose dad isn't in the picture?"

"Give the gentleman a cigar!" Melanie put up her hand to give Mac a high five. (And instantly realized, I need to calm down a bit, pronto.)

Mac had only wanted to have his lunch in peace. He wasn't looking for this, but here he was, sharing a lunchtime conversation with someone who needed a friend. And for some inexplicable reason, he couldn't bring himself to respond in the affirmative to Melanie's invitation to be sarcastic about the fact that she had a child.

"Look, I'm sorry... Boy or girl?"

"Girl."

"Looks like you then?"

"Actually, she looks like her father, but she acts a lot like me."

"Then you must be proud of her."

"What do you mean?"

"Because she's fearless."

Melanie shot a quizzical look at Mac, so he continued. "Her mom isn't afraid to come up to a complete stranger, and strike up a conversation in the middle of a workplace cafeteria."

"Maybe her mom is immensely frazzled at the moment."

"Maybe her mom is being immensely honest."

So, thought Melanie, as she took a quick sideways glance at the clock on the cafeteria wall. I've got five minutes to wrap this up. Do I pass along my phone number to Mac? Would that be too forward? Do I let him know that I appreciate what he just said, sticking up for a total stranger, and then leave the ball in his court? Or do I take the coward's way out and say, "nice chatting with you, gotta get back to work?"

At the same moment Mac was thinking that having the beginnings of an intimate conversation with an associate had been the last thing on his mind when he sat down to lunch. But instead, he had gotten placed in the middle of Melanie's life.

He could ask for her phone number, but would that appear too bold? He could just write his work number down and noncommittally pass it along, saying something like, "if you ever want to talk about it, I'm a member of the team resource crew," keeping it strictly work related? Or he could take an end run over the whole possibility of a relationship forming by saying something like, "you strike me as being a person who has more than enough ability to figure things out, I know it'll be ok," and then quickly smile, stand up and walk away?

Normally, Mac wasn't much of risk taker, and it would have been extremely easy for him to choose option three. Instead he looked directly at Melanie and smiled before saying: "How would you like to have dinner together some time? How difficult is getting a babysitter?"

Melanie smiled back: "How's Saturday? That's normally when Moxie spends time with my mom and dad." She wrote down her phone number and handed it to Mac.

"Moxie?" He raised his eyebrows and his smile became even broader.

"I should warn you, she's a real character."

"Guess she gets that from her mom, too?"

"Yeah," nodded Melanie, "she does."

Lincoln

It was bad enough that she had been named after a famous guy-type person. But with a name like Lincoln, everyone expected you to be wise, or at least tall and lanky, and she was none of that. But she was a great storyteller, so at least she had that in common with Honest Abe.

Lincoln Meade was every bit of five foot three inches tall, with deep brown eyes and reddish blonde hair. Although she had attended 12 years of Parochial (as in Catholic) school at Our Lady of the Lake, she had been providentially spared most of its side-effects.

In fact, on several occasions while growing up, after expressing an alternate opinion that heaven wasn't reserved solely for them, Lincoln had been directed to the principal's office, where Mother Mary Martin had listened to her theological treatise.

"So, Miss Meade, are we at it again?"

"I guess so, Mother."

"Do you have anything new to add to your argument?"

"Actually Mother, I do."

"Let's hear it then."

"I've been thinking about the Ninety-five Theses."

"Go on."

To be fair, it was the late 1980s and things were beginning to loosen up a bit, so Martin Luther was no longer considered the archenemy of Holy Mother the Church. But Mother Mary had come to look forward to her time spent with Lincoln, being kind enough to appreciate another's point of view, even if her own sisterhood got in the way of it.

"Number sixty-two is my current favorite."

"Which is that one?"

"The main treasure of the church should be the gospels and the grace of God."

"Sounds reasonable, doesn't it?"

"It does, but that's why I was kicked out of class. Sister Terese thought I was being spiritually uppity."

"What exactly did she tell you?"

"She said there's plenty more to our religion than Matthew, Mark, Luke and John could possibly have known. And that lots of people needed plenary indulgences to get into heaven, so indulgences were actually an outward sign of God's grace towards us."

At this remark, Mother Mary had raised her eyebrows. "Then what did you say?"

"I mentioned that Matthew, Mark, Luke and John weren't Catholic. Most of them were Jews who decided to follow Jesus, who also happened to be a Jew. Which is what got me kicked out of class."

"I see."

"But I'd actually been thinking about it a lot Mother, and as far as I can tell, Jesus didn't sell anything, especially not his forgiveness. That's what got Martin Luther so worked up about plenary indulgences."

"Worked up?"

"Frustrated enough to sit down and write ninety-five things that he thought were important that the Church in Rome wasn't following."

"I can tell that you're a bit frustrated as well, Miss Meade."

Lincoln took Mother Mary's observation as an invitation to continue the conversation. "I think number ninety-four is right up there with the best of them."

"Which one is that?"

"Christians must follow Christ at all costs."

"And what do you suppose that means?"

"Being a follower of Jesus should cost us something. It's not a totally free arrangement. I mean, grace and mercy are things that we definitely don't earn. I think that was what caused Luther to think that something about the Church wasn't right. He pointed out that we're saved by grace. But he didn't mean to imply that everything else would be easy."

"For instance?"

"For instance, as a follower of Jesus I'm supposed to save my body for my future husband. But most of the time that's not an easy thing to do. In fact, you'd be surprised how many kids at Our Lady of the Lake think that's open to interpretation."

Mother Mary stifled a smile. She's an honest one, she thought. And if there was one thing that Mother Mary had learned in her 25 years of being a principal, it was that an honest student was one that appreciated open communication.

"Did you know that one of the Theses actually covers this very thing?" Lincoln continued.

"Go on."

"Number seventy-two. 'Blessed are they who think about being forgiven.' Luther knew that if you were thinking about being forgiven that your conscience was still in a state of being used by God to bring you back."

"So he was condoning sin?"

'No. It was more that he knew how God works within us. As long as we're open to the Holy Spirit, it's our own conscience that motivates us to seek God's forgiveness, which is freely given."

Lincoln sat up straight for emphasis, as if she were making the final point in her summation to the jury. "If this is the case, then there truly was no need for the church to grant an indulgence for sins based on a person's ability to pay."

Mother Mary was impressed. Since Lincoln was turning out to be a regular visitor in her office during senior year, Mother

Mary actually had reached the point where she looked forward to their conversations. She smiled before offering a response.

"Between you and me, I understand your logic, Miss Meade. But thinking thoroughly about what everyone else accepts without thinking often upsets the applecart."

Lincoln smiled back. "So do you have any suggestions for me? I mean, I'm not trying to cause a problem for Sister Terese."

"Miss Meade, God has given you a very keen mind. As you get older, I'm very sure that He'll give you the wisdom to realize when it's best to put forth an argument, and when it's best to let it go for another day."

As a 42-year-old, looking back on the experience, Lincoln knew that her conversation with Mother Mary had been a defining moment. Mother Mary had given Lincoln an opportunity to safely speak her mind without branding her a heretic.

Lincoln was sitting in the law office where she worked, looking out the window. She was brought back to reality when Hillary, the paralegal assigned to her, knocked on the door before walking in.

"Everything ok?" Hillary asked as she placed a file on the desk.

"Yes. Thanks!"

"The judge called to reschedule the defense's rebuttal for tomorrow at two. Which means we can go over the research I found later in the morning, if you want."

"That's good. Thank you."

Hillary could sense that Lincoln's mind was elsewhere, so she excused herself. After a few seconds of going through the file, Lincoln was back on memory lane. This time she was a freshman at Hunter Community College, working in the audio-visual department with Abigail, who was a feisty elementary education major. It was late afternoon and they were the only two left in the office, filing away requests for equipment. Somehow the conversation got around to religion.

"So, do you believe in God?" Lincoln had asked.

"Of course! I'm a Seventh Day Adventist," Abigail had answered, full of conviction.

At that point in her life, Lincoln had never met someone of that particular persuasion.

"What sort of things does your religion teach?"

"Well, we believe that the Seventh Day Adventist religion is the one true expression of Christianity, and God used Ellen White to help bring Christians back to the truth."

"Wow!" was Lincoln's first response. "I was raised a Catholic, and we were taught that we're the one true faith too! Isn't that fantastic?!"

"How is that fantastic?" Abigail responded.

"I mean, both Seventh Day Adventists and Catholics believe that their faith is the only legitimate one. They can't both be right."

"Exactly. That's why ours is the true way."

"But how do you know that?"

"Because Ellen White received a direct revelation from God about it."

"But Catholics can trace their leadership back to Saint Peter. That's why they believe that the Pope is infallible." (By this point in her life, Lincoln was no longer practicing, but she enjoyed 'theological explorations,' as she called them.)

Abigail looked at Lincoln a minute before answering. "No one but God is infallible. It's pretty convenient for a religion to say that their leader can't be mistaken on matters of faith, don't you think?"

"Sure, and it's just as convenient for anyone who is dissatisfied with the current state of affairs to claim that they had a divine revelation of something different. I think it's good to have an open mind about this sort of thing, don't you?"

At that point Abigail had steered the direction of the conversation away from religion, leaving Lincoln feeling disappointed.

A few years later, Lincoln was cleaning her apartment

when she answered a knock on the door. It was two Mormon missionaries, well-scrubbed, wearing white shirts, black ties and black trousers, with sincere smiles on their faces.

"Good morning!" said the taller of the two. "We're from the Latter Day Saints and wondered if we could take a moment of your time?"

Lincoln readily agreed.

"Have you read the Book of Mormon, by any chance?"

"No, but I've heard about it."

"Then you may know that we believe that the Book of Mormon was divinely inspired when Joseph Smith received a visitation from an angel sent from God," said the shorter of the two.

"So God felt He had to add something to the Bible?"

"Basically. The initial revelation from the New Testament wasn't complete."

This struck Lincoln as sort of odd, but interesting. "So Jesus needed some help after He died, was resurrected and ascended into heaven?"

At this point the shorter of the two's smile became even broader. This guy has amazing teeth, thought Lincoln. In fact, they both do!

"It's not like Jesus needed help, it's more like God knew the human race needed time to wait for further instructions," said the taller of the two, whose smile also widened.

"So, your basic point is that we, as humans, should be ready to receive additional revelation as to the completeness of God, at any point in our history?"

"That's a good way of putting it," said the shorter of the two.

This struck Lincoln as being very funny, but out of respect, she tried to stifle a laugh. Which proved to be a mistake because she wound up putting her hand to mouth and sort of snorted, which caught her guests off guard.

"I always thought that God was pretty complete, as is. And that if Jesus is God's son, then Jesus' life should sum up the totality of God for us. Not to mention I remember somewhere in the New Testament where Jesus told his apostles that He'd send the Holy Spirit to help explain things."

She took a deep breath, waiting for her statement to sink in a bit before she continued. What came out of her mouth next actually surprised her: "Would you mind if I prayed for all of us to receive a deeper appreciation for God?"

Much to her delight, and because she had asked to pray to God and not His Son, the two missionaries nodded their heads in the affirmative. They actually closed their eyes as Lincoln prayed a short prayer. Afterwards they shook hands before leaving, giving Lincoln a copy of their book.

It was highly ironic that just two days later, she was on a city bus, headed downtown, skimming through the Book of Mormon. Lincoln wondered how she was going to get it back to them when who should come on the bus but her two Mormon friends.

"Hey guys!" she spoke up, motioning for them to sit next to her as she handed the book back. "Thank you for the loan!"

Lincoln went to the law office break room, fetched her take-out container of noodles with peanut sauce, and put it in the microwave. She always ordered it before litigation because of the protein and the fact that she liked most anything to do with peanuts. As she was waiting for her lunch to warm up, one more memory came to her.

It had happened a few years before her encounter with the Mormons. She was with her mom at home and they had just put supper on the table, when a knock came from the front door. It was funny how God orchestrated these things, she thought. Lincoln moved from the kitchen and found a young looking man on the front porch.

"Hi! I'm Pastor Wesley, from the Baptist Church a few blocks from here. And I wondered if this is a good time for me to come in and introduce our church to you?"

Lincoln didn't hesitate to call out: "Mom, Pastor Wesley would like to speak with us. What do you say?"

Her mom Amanda, was always up for a conversation, especially at dinner time. Amanda had been raised an evangelical Lutheran in a small town, but as she grew older, she gradually exchanged the formalities of religion for an emphasis on the heart of the matter itself. So she called back: "Why not? Ask him if he's had his supper yet."

Wesley smiled at the invitation. It turned out he had skipped lunch because it was his day to do 'house round-ups,' as he called them: cold-calling on folks within a three mile radius of his church. So he was very happy to sit down to a meal of comfort food.

"So, Pastor Wesley," said Amanda, passing the mashed potatoes. "What exactly do Baptists believe?"

"We put God's word above everything else," he said, eyeing the meatloaf as it came his way. "To us, God's word is sovereign. The ultimate authority. And God's word tells us that it's important to have a personal relationship with Him. Especially since we're living in a time of extreme darkness."

"Isn't that a little harsh of an assessment?" asked Lincoln, looking at her mother mischievously. "I mean, if I'm understanding you correctly, you seem to be placing a lot of emphasis on one book that was written by people."

"It's God's word we're talking about," answered Wesley, trying his best to be polite as well as determined. "And God's word is nothing but the truth. We believe that the Bible was divinely inspired, so everything outside of His word is subject to interpretation."

"But that view, in itself, could be considered an interpretation, right?" said Lincoln. "Having an open mind about this sort of thing is very important. It keeps a person hungry for the truth."

"An open mind, in general, is a good thing, but it can also be a trap. How can you distinguish anything as ultimate unless you make a decision to reach a conclusion? By definition, an open mind is a revolving door that keeps truth out."

This time Lincoln smiled. Baptists must care enough to send their future pastors to first-class seminaries, she thought. At least ones that spent some time on apologetics. Other than stimulating meal-time conversation, what was the point of it, long-term? It reminded Lincoln of the time she had volunteered at a local soup kitchen, and one rainy afternoon, in between cleaning up after the lunch crowd and getting supper ready, she got caught in the middle of a conversation between two regulars from the neighborhood, each adamant that they knew the one true God. It wasn't as if Lincoln was a relativist, but if there ever was a case for it, those two were surely making it.

Lincoln continued: "In the end, it's what Jesus' apostles did in interacting with their neighbors that spread the Gospel. The Book of Acts is just filled with examples of it."

"Pastor Wesley, would you care for some homemade lattice crust cherry pie with vanilla ice cream?" Amanda smiled sweetly, looking Wesley directly in the eye, doing her best to intervene.

Wesley was overjoyed to accept. Dessert was spent chatting about less confrontational subjects.

"I've really enjoyed our conversation and the dinner. Thank you!" Wesley said as he got up from the table. "Would you like help with the dishes?"

Amanda thought: What an exceptionally well-bred Midwestern boy. But then the thought came, maybe he's just being polite to pick up spiritual brownie-points? "No. But thank you Wesley for the offer."

Lincoln finished her noodles with peanut sauce and washed the container for future use. Her memories had taken her for quite a ride since coming in to work that morning. As she tossed her napkin away and headed back down the hall to her office, a final Thesis, Luther's second one to be exact, came to mind. It was one that seemed to sum up the whole subject of religion for her: "Only God can give salvation."

Persistence

Jessica was sitting in Central Park, just across the street from the Plaza Hotel. It was a mid-November day and unusually mild, sunny and absolutely perfect for people watching. Soon, her eyes became focused on a young Hispanic mother and her daughter, who appeared to be about three.

The mom had sat down on a bench across from Jessica. She was attempting to zip up her daughter's jacket, but each time, the daughter pushed her hands away. "Let me do it!" she said, trying to zip it. Mother and daughter went back and forth for a minute, each time the daughter nudging her mother's hands away, until finally, the daughter was successful. As she zipped up the jacket, a huge smile crossed her mouth.

"Mommy! I did it!" she said proudly.

"Yes you did Bella! You sure did!" said the mom.

"Wow," thought Jessica. "Why can't I be persistent like that?"

Suddenly in rapid-fire sequence, images flashed across her mind. Images that were her mind's way of trying to answer what could have happened if she had been more persistent.

In the first image, Jessica was in fifth grade. It was the year that she found herself attracted to Matt, a boy who was shorter than the rest of her classmates and quieter. She had just moved with her family from California, and she was having trouble making friends in the small Midwestern town where her father had been transferred. At any rate, she had tried to start up conversations with Matt in hopes of pursuing a friendship.

She had wanted to make friends in the worst possible way. Back in California, she hadn't had a problem, but kids in the Midwest didn't seem to be as open. The problem was that Matt wasn't much of a talker, which for some reason made him more attractive to Jessica. Maybe it was subconscious affiliation, or just plain curiosity. But she couldn't seem to get him out of his shell. Until the day that he, on his own, turned to her and said, "Hey Jessica, I want to show you something!"

Matt was clearly proud of whatever it was he was about to show her. Jessica was thrilled to have him initiate a conversation.

"I'd like to see it," she said, smiling.

He smiled back and pulled out a pocket knife. "It's brand new!" he said, "A real beauty!"

Instantly a wave of disappointment came over Jessica. "Oh Matt, how could you!"

It was flowing out of 11 year-old female disappointment. How could a boy who had seemed to her to be so nice, turn out to have something she found so repulsive to show her? Jessica's young mind couldn't make sense of it. Matt clearly understood that something had happened between them, that he had somehow let Jessica down, but he hadn't a clue how to address it. So the two of them never spoke again and at the end of the school year her family moved back to California.

Looking back on it now, Jessica was impressed with the fact that it only took an instant for her to do a complete emotional make-over with Matt, moving from infatuation to revulsion. And the thing that caused such the 180-degree turn was actually quite small, and had nothing to do with Matt. It wasn't as if he said something unkind. It wasn't as if he had mistreated her. It wasn't as if he had done anything that young boys typically do to cover up affection towards a female.

What if she had told Matt, early on, that she liked him? Before letting it build up, adding unnecessary significance to the pocket knife episode? What if he had possessed the ability to articulate his sensitivity? The fact was, Matt was just as attracted to Jessica as she had been to him. All he had to say was, "I'm sorry," or "What's wrong? It's only a pocket knife."

At least she would have had an opportunity to tell him how she felt. And their relationship could have ended on a much different note.

Instead of not talking, they would have shared lunch times together. And by the time Jessica's family had moved back to California, they would have been close friends – as only girls and boys can be before the complication of hormones gets in the way. They would have written to each other. They would have continued to share secrets through a long-distance relationship that could have resulted in their seeing each other over summers.

And then the image came to Jessica of a scene from high school. She had been a junior. Liam was a senior. Jessica was walking along the second floor corridor, on her way to leaving the building. As she passed one of the classrooms, she heard Liam's laugh. They were both in journalism class and worked on the school newspaper. He was the assistant editor and had to approve all copy. So he was always focused on the story when she sat across from him, but slowly she found herself becoming attracted to him. His helpfulness, his smile, and the way he had of being himself with her that made him stand out. Because he wasn't thinking of Jessica in terms of dating, he was completely at ease with her. Oftentimes, Jessica thought, "how on earth is it possible that he isn't even aware of how I'm feeling towards him?"

But the two of them were never alone. Liam looked over her copy and offered suggestions only in the classroom. So there was no chance for much personal conversation. The fact that Liam wrote poetry and the editor of the newspaper chose to publish some of the poems in the last edition only was icing on the cake. The poems he had written were about unrequited love. And ironically, they were written for another girl who was a senior.

But as far as Jessica was concerned, they might as well have been written for her. In fact, she authored a poem of her own that was published in the very same issue, titled "It Might Have Been." And she had penned it for him.

So when she heard Liam's laughter coming from the classroom, with only one week left in the school year, she decided to go for it. Jessica walked into the room and found Liam hanging out with his best friend Roger. They were both on the track team and were supposed to be running stairs before heading outside to the track. Liam's mind was totally on joking mode. Roger was a tremendously witty person and he had a way of bringing out the fun in him.

As Jessica walked in. Liam turned towards her.

"Hi," she said tentatively.

"What's up Jessica?"

"I wanted to ask you something."

How do you ask a boy to pay attention to you she thought. How do I ask him out with another boy in the room? It'd be bad enough to get rejected with no one seeing it. But to have a witness was too much. Jessica had to make a quick decision.

"I… I…" she stammered. This was not coming out at all like I want it to, she thought. "Can I talk with you sometime?"

Roger nudged Liam in the ribs. "We gotta get going," he said as he began to walk out of the room.

Liam looked at Jessica for a moment, but not long enough. He didn't see the invitation to friendship in her eyes. He didn't see the anticipation. He couldn't see a young woman's longing to share her heart with him.

"Sure," he said. "Maybe later, ok? I should really get back to practice."

Jessica was too let down to say anything else. Can't he see that I care for him? she thought.

Three weeks later, school was over. Liam graduated and moved on, without ever speaking to Jessica again.

I should have said something, thought Jessica.

What if I had begun with, "Wait a minute! This really can't wait."

"What is it?"

"I may not have another chance, so I'm just going to come out and say it. All this year I've wanted to get to know you. I mean, you and I have been in the same class and you've helped me with my writing and, you know those poems you wrote in the last issue of our newspaper?"

"Yes, sure."

"I loved them."

"Well, thanks. I appreciate that."

"I mean, I loved them because I felt they were written to me."

"Why would you think that?"

"Because the poem I had published was written to you."

Liam's eyes would have opened wide. He would have immediately registered the way that Jessica was feeling towards him.

"Jessica, I had no idea. I mean, you wrote a great poem. But the reason I understood it was because I was feeling the same way... about someone else."

"Who didn't seem to know that you existed?"

"Sort of."

"Who didn't have a clue about how you truly felt because you were afraid to take a chance and tell her?"

"Basically."

"Because they were dense as a rain forest?"

Liam would have laughed out loud.

"Good image!"

"Thanks, I normally go for sarcasm when romance doesn't work out."

"I am so sorry Jessica. I really am. Why didn't you say something sooner?"

"Do you know how hard it is for a junior of the female persuasion to speak up to a senior of the male persuasion about anything? Especially if it involves feelings? Most especially if it involves feelings that might be unrequited?"

"Actually, I do. I mean, about the feelings part."

"And guys can be..."

"Pretty slow on the uptake. So you were sitting across from me, watching me read your poem, realizing that I had no clue."

"What was I supposed to do, title it, 'Hey Liam, Notice Me Will Ya?"

"Not a very romantic title."

Jessica couldn't have helped but laugh, despite herself.

"Not very, but it would have been accurate."

Liam would have smiled at her. "So, are you angry with me?"

She would have shaken her head 'no' before answering. "More like frustrated. Really, really frustrated."

"Frustrated, as in you're going to get in your car and try to run me over?"

"Pretty much. So, tell me something; your poems in the newspaper, they'd indicate that you aren't currently dating, right?"

"Right."

"But you're attracted to a certain person of the opposite gender."

"Fair assumption."

"So how does that make you feel?"

Liam would have laughed. Jessica had him on the ropes. If he admitted that he felt awful, she could counter with, 'how ironic,' or if he said it didn't really bother him because it was all in the past, she could go for the 'what is it with guys anyway? You screw up with one girl and make the rest of us pay for it?' approach.

But he surprised himself and said, "I'd rather you tell me how badly I hurt you."

Jessica was taken aback. "Are you being serious?"

"Look, I know we aren't best friends, but I hope that you

know me well enough after being in class together all year to understand that I would never, ever hurt you on purpose."

"Yeah, I know that."

"Then please tell me, how badly did I mess up?"

She looked Liam directly in the eye. "I was thinking about hiring an attorney."

"You're thinking of suing me?"

"For lack of interest, which led to extreme frustration, which resulted in diminished performance on my finals."

He laughed again. "Wow, are you already thinking pre-law?"

She couldn't help herself: "It's never too early. You remember what Walt Whitman suggested."

"I can't say that I do."

"Out of the cradle, endlessly rocking, out of the courthouse, endlessly litigating..."

It was Liam who brought the conversation back home. "Well, please don't sue me."

"Why not? I could make a small fortune, maybe pay my way through college."

"I'd rather you didn't."

"Don't you like a good knock down drag out fight? You're Italian, right?"

"Yeah, and with a name like O'Malley, you enjoy a good public confrontation every now and then?"

"I'm also part Welsh. Exactly half and half."

"What is Wales noted for anyway?"

Jessica didn't miss a beat: "Beautiful blue-eyed maidens. And when combined with the Celtic influence, they tend to be very musical and like to dance a lot."

"So the bottom line is that women who are half Irish are a lot of fun to be around."

"Ordinarily, when their boyfriends aren't jilting them."

Then Liam would have asked Jessica out. They would have gotten a corner booth, where they could have continued their conversation and gotten to know each other. All the time Jessica would have been feeling like she was walking on air. She had been given a second chance and the feelings that she had held inside for an entire school year were being validated, big time.

For his part, Liam would have spent most of the time realizing that Jessica had the most gorgeous eyes he had ever seen. Her eyes were warm and inviting and teasing and compassionate all at once.

Then, still sitting there in Central Park, on a whim, Jessica pulled out her smartphone and googled "Liam Asperelli." She found one who was an attorney, working for the Southern Poverty Law Center. The same Liam had two sons and had been divorced ten years. And he had lived in southern California where they had both attended high school. "This really could be him!" she thought. She looked up the Southern Poverty Law Center's phone number and called. Jessica was put on hold, but after a minute, Liam came to the phone.

"Liam speaking. Can I help you?"

She could barely breathe.

"Hello?" he asked.

Jessica felt like she was about to faint, but she held on for dear life. "I'm trying to reach Liam Asperelli."

"Speaking."

It was him but it still felt surreal. "Would you by any chance be interested in a blind date?"

"Pardon?"

"A blind date. At least in part."

"Excuse me, but you're not making a whole lot of sense, ma'am."

"I was wondering if you wrote much poetry lately?"

He laughed at the reference. "Actually, I wrote some pretty bad stuff back in high school. But there was this beautiful girl who wrote some amazing verse."

"Oh, really?"

"Yes. Exceptionally evocative. Wise beyond her years."

"Sounds like she really made an impact on you."

"She did. More than she'll ever know."

"What do you mean?"

"I mean I was young and stupid, and the last time we were together, she was trying to ask me something. But I was just too ignorant to appreciate it."

"Appreciate what?"

"That she might have been wanting to go deeper in the relationship, and I blew her off, because I didn't realize that sometimes you only get one opportunity."

"That's pretty fatalistic, isn't it?"

Liam didn't know why, but he was enjoying talking to this woman, even if he didn't know her.

"Well, isn't it sort of obvious? I'm talking about an exceptional woman who I could have gotten to know twenty years ago, but it didn't work out. We went our separate ways and that's that."

"You sure there isn't more to the story?"

"Like what for instance?"

"Like maybe she grew up to be a therapist and realized that she could have been more persistent."

"O.K., sure, I suppose that's possible, but why even spend good time hashing over something that's in the past?"

"Maybe the past just skyrocketed itself into the present."

"Now it's my turn to ask: What do you mean?"

"I mean what if I told you that I knew this person and how to get in touch with her?"

"Look, I'm sorry, but we're talking about something that happened a long time ago."

"Will you let me describe her?"

"Be my guest."

"This girl you're talking about was about five feet, two inches tall, with blue eyes, reddish blonde hair. Definitely Irish looking. How am I doing so far?"

"Go on."

"And she had quite a sense of humor. She could tease the tears off a baby."

"That actually sounds like something she would have said."

"That's because she's saying it. It's Jessica O'Malley."

Silence. About 15 full seconds of it passed between them. Enough to seem like a lifetime. Emotions are fleeting and precariously inaccurate indicators of reality. So how do you respond when life hands you a second chance when your heart seems to be thumping along at a hundred miles an hour?

"How badly did I treat you?"

The question caught Jessica off guard. "Pardon?"

"Are you calling me to get even or to pick up where we left off?" His lawyer's instinct figured it had to be one or the other. There was no in-between after 20 years.

For some reason, just hearing Liam's voice brought out the teasing part of her. "Hey Liam, Notice Me Will Ya?" She laughed out loud at her reference to the poem she had written long ago.

"I absolutely promise."

The Artificial Conception

Tim McTavish was fairly frustrated. In fact, if there were one word that could have succinctly summed up his life at this point, it would have been: frustrated.

He'd had it with monumental inaction on the relationship front. So much so that he decided to print out a bunch of "Do You Believe In True Love? If so, and you're female, and interested, I live in the grey Cape Cod at the end of the street" flyers on his computer and dropped one off at each door on his block.

So, seeing as it was a middle-of-the-winter type day, around 28 degrees but felt like minus five due to the chill factor, he bundled up, went outside and spent exactly 27 minutes dropping off a flyer at each house that didn't have a tell-tale sign of marriage. Which meant that he was hitting every home, because marriage, even though it's supposed to be the most important relationship two humans can have with each other on earth, doesn't often leave obvious signs of its existence.

Actually, I'm digressing just a smidgeon, because I forgot to tell you that 18 houses down the block on the left, McTavish literally ran into a woman who knocked him down as she made a run from the house to her car to retrieve her cell phone.

The funny thing about cell phones was that McTavish didn't believe in them. "Cell phones coerce a person into trading their freedom for the illusion of safety," he'd say. "I'm not so afraid of being stranded that I force myself to be available to people twenty-four hours a day."

He wasn't the most sociable person on the planet.

The name of the person who accidentally upended McTavish was Abby Herzog. Abby was the director of an advertising agency and she had a 10 year-old daughter, Audrey, who liked to be called Archie. Whenever Abby was in a hurry, she tended to talk in ad-speak. Depending upon the situation, her conversation had a tendency to get rather clipped.

For instance, at 8:26 on a Saturday morning when she had a big meeting first thing on Monday about the Helderson campaign, and Audrey was being her usual early-morning chirpy self:

"So Mom, what's the haps?"

"What?"

"What've you got lined up today?"

"Sorry honey, distracted a bit, gotta clear the deck for the battle."

"What battle?"

"There's a real snoozer of a campaign that one of our clients wants us to turn around."

"So, that's a good thing, right?"

"Honey, the poor guy's drowning in clichés."

"But that's good for you Mom. More work, right?"

"Yeah. Sure. Eeny, meeny, miny, moe, catch a slogan by its toe."

"Hey Mom, that's pretty good! You should use that."

"Stop it."

"I'm serious!"

"Come on."

"Mom, you should go with the flow on this one."

"The 'flow'? Sweetie, no slogan isn't a slogan."

"No slogan is the new slogan Mom, that's just it!"

"Stop it."

"No, you stop it! Quit being negative and listen."

"Honey, I'm not going to run that one up the pole and see if they'll salute."

"Why not? It's cute."

"Rome wasn't built in a day, sweetie."

"So?"

"Things that last take time."

"Like relationships?"

"Like ad campaigns!"

Getting back to McTavish, after Abby knocked him over, she looked him up and down very slowly without apologizing.

"Can I help you?" she opted for the sarcastic approach. It wasn't her fault that it was a defense mechanism that worked something like ninety-nine percent of the time.

"No thanks. I'm pretty sure the snow cover has taken care of a potential broken hip and besides, I'd have to know your name in order to sue you," he shot back.

Maybe it was the cold air, or maybe it was the fact that she had been in such a hurry to make a phone call she didn't want to make, or maybe it was the way that McTavish's lip was profusely bleeding that caused Abby to switch gears.

"Hey, geez, I'm sorry. Do you want to come in and let me patch you up?"

"Do I look like I require surgery?"

McTavish had no idea he was losing blood.

"You must have hit your lip on something on the way down after we bumped into each other. Why don't you let me look at it? If you need an operation, I can call 911."

"Sure. Thank you."

Audrey had been looking out the front window and saw the whole thing. By the time her Mom and McTavish had gotten to the porch, Audrey had opened the front door to let them in.

"Just sit over there on the couch and let me get a warm washcloth," said Abby, as she went to the bathroom to fetch one.

As McTavish sat down he took notice of Audrey's dark

brown hair and the way her eyebrows arched up as their eyes met.

"Aren't you the guy who lives down the street, on the corner, with the slate-gray vinyl siding and cranberry red shutters?"

"That would be me."

"Cute house. At least from the outside. Are you always this clumsy?"

"Not under normal circumstances."

"Any kids?"

"No, not that I know of."

"What's that supposed to mean?"

"Nothing."

"Everything means something."

At this point Abby walked back into the living room and placed the washcloth over McTavish's mouth.

"Honey, that's brilliant!"

"What?"

"'Everything means something!' That's exactly what we'll use for the Helderson campaign."

At this point McTavish thought he should speak up or get lost in the conversation.

"So, I'm feeling better already. Funny how a little R and R will work wonders. It was nice to meet you."

He got up to leave, but Abby wasn't having it. "Why did you stop at my house?"

"Yeah," Audrey backed her mother up, "and what is it that you're handing out to everyone?"

Audrey's visual capabilities were along the lines of an eagle. Being bored with her Cheerios, she had been slumped over the living room couch, looking out the window for signs of intelligent life on the block and had noticed McTavish slowly working his way down the street.

"Right, come to think of it, what were you trying to hand me before we ran into each other?" asked Abby.

McTavish felt like he was being sucked into an alternate

universe, one that required conversation and human interaction, and it was way too early in the morning to consider it. His eyes made a darting glance towards the front door as he summoned all the energy he currently held in his body. "I'm feeling much better. Thank you for your hospitality, really, I'm all set."

He got up to move. Audrey was on the case. "No you're not."

"Pardon?"

"You're not ready to leave. Your face is chalky white, like you're in shock," said Abby, "Honey, I'm going to get our neighbor a little something to eat. Can you keep him company?"

"Sure Mom, I don't have any homework for the weekend anyway."

Audrey was a real super-helper. The kind of kid that every mom dreams of having. Sweet, kind, smart as a whip, funny and naturally upbeat. She couldn't have asked for a better daughter. Too bad Abby couldn't say exactly how much of those traits came from the father. But that's the way it goes, she rationalized, sometimes God works a miracle and rearranges our DNA to make up for certain factors.

Besides being helpful, Audrey was also inquisitive, which led to her fascination with books and learning. In fact, Audrey couldn't get enough homework. She had already skipped two grades in her five years in elementary school. She preferred the company of adults, except that they, by and large, didn't seem to have much of a sense of humor. That was another thing about Audrey – she loved to laugh. Not just your normal, ha-ha sort of chuckle either. When she laughed, she practically exploded. Her laugh was from someplace deep inside, a wellspring of happiness that couldn't be stopped.

Once Abby was safely out of conversational range, Audrey took advantage of her window of opportunity to interrogate her neighbor.

"So, remind me again why you were stopping at every house on the block?"

"I was conducting a social experiment."

Just then her laugh kicked in. "On your neighbors?"

"What neighbors? Can you honestly say that you know who lives on this block?"

Audrey was too smart to put up with this line of questioning. "Look, I only want to know what the heck you were doing, that's all. I saw the piece of paper you were going to give my mom. Fork it over, please."

"It's personal."

"Of course it's personal, why else would you be out going door to door in the middle of winter?"

Wow, thought McTavish. This kid is razor sharp, mach ten. I could try to make a break for it right now before her mother comes back, but the kid would track me down and make it worse. I could tell her I'm in grad school and had to conduct a psychology experiment. But she'd ask me too many follow-up questions. So, in the long run, maybe it's best to get it out in the open.

And just as McTavish was about to spill the beans, Abby came back in the room with a bagel and cream cheese and a cup of coffee. "I can get you tea or water if you'd rather," she said half apologizing for her new-found hospitality. Now that she'd had a moment to think about it, having McTavish in her living room wasn't that bad. She'd seen him walking down the street to the park often enough. He seemed to be on a mission. She'd wondered why he was walking so quickly, like he was in a hurry to get it over with.

"Thank you, the coffee's great."

McTavish took a bite of the bagel and took a good look at Abby. She was alarmingly cute. Medium cut, dark brown curly hair. Beautiful hazel eyes.

"You've stopped bleeding. That's a good sign," she told him.

At this point Abby took another look at McTavish. She guessed he was about ten years older than she was, but nature had been kind to him. He wore wire-rimmed glasses that framed brown eyes. He had thick salt-and-pepper hair, and was, to tell the truth, a little on the short side. She decided that he looked like a middle-aged Peter Falk, maybe a year or so after his Columbo phase.

This was a good thing because Abby had been a huge Columbo fan growing up. So what if they were reruns? She hadn't seen them before, and besides, 1990's television was pretty much a wasteland for a teenager. Anyway, it wasn't often that a semi-stranger from down the block wound up in her living room, and the guy seemed harmless enough and actually slightly interesting. Forget the Helderson campaign, she thought, it's Saturday; let's see where this goes.

"So, do you mind if I ask, what's your name?" Abby didn't have her daughter's detective instincts, but, sometimes a direct question gets the same result as deduction.

"Tim. Tim McTavish. And you?"

"Abby Herzog. So, Tim, my daughter and I are dying to know what you were doing before we got up close and personal."

"Speak for yourself, Mom. I actually know what Mr. McTavish was up to."

"Really sweetie?"

This has got to be good, thought Abby. Besides being bright and funny and helpful, Audrey was gifted with an impressive imagination that didn't need much priming. Especially if it involved the potential for true love. Unbeknownst to McTavish, he had inadvertently stumbled upon a home within which all occupants believed in it. Despite Abby's strong desire to spare her daughter the heartache of going after such an unattainable thing, she herself couldn't help it. Even though she'd had to settle for artificial insemination.

As far as Audrey was concerned, her mother had satisfactorily explained her somewhat irregular conception when she was eight years old. Of course, it wasn't Abby who had brought up the subject. It was Christmas Eve and they had just finished watching "It's A Wonderful Life." For both mother and daughter the telephone scene said it all. (You know the one where George

Bailey and Mary Hatch are listening to Sam Wainwright explain how they can get in on the ground floor, and George and Mary keep inching closer to each other, and George tells Sam Wainwright he doesn't want to get in on the ground floor. Then he drops the phone and Mary and George stare into each other's eyes, and George tells Mary that he wants to get the heck out of Bedford Falls, but Mary looks at him like she's not hearing those words at all. And before you know it, they're kissing each other because they've fallen in love.)

The irony of Abby's life was that she'd managed to keep that spark of true love inside her, despite several relationships that could only be classified as duds.

So, on that fateful Christmas Eve, Audrey had reacted to the news of how her conception had come about in a pretty straightforward way. "Mom, that is totally awesome!" In typical Audrey fashion, she began to piece the puzzle together. No wonder she had such a strong-willed approach to love and relationships. In Audrey's mind, you were either in love, or you weren't. You either were in a relationship with someone, or you weren't. The middle ground of being 'just friends' didn't exist. There was no room for ambiguity, and this played itself out in Audrey's every action. She was the sort of girl who was passionate to a fault. No one was Audrey's secret friend. If she liked you, you knew it.

"Yeah," said Audrey. "I actually know what Mr. McTavish is up to. Number one, it's winter out there. He wouldn't be walking door to door unless it was super important. Number two, he very clearly wants every house on the block to know what he's after because he's written it down for them. Number three, he's not too keen on verbal communication, at least not initially. But that's got to be frustrating for him because he obviously has a lot on his mind. How am I doing so far?"

"Nicely put, especially the part about being frustrated," said McTavish.

"Thanks, but all those things are pretty obvious. The fourth thing coming up is sort of speculation. Do you mind if I go on?"

"Be my guest."

"So whatever is bothering you is pretty deep. In fact, it'd have to be about the deepest thing that you could want to express. Why else would you suddenly choose to become Mr. Sociable when it's below zero out there?"

Audrey paused for a second, got up from the couch and walked over to McTavish. "Actually, what's motivating you isn't frustration at all. I mean, frustration isn't an emotion that engages people towards positive action. What's motivating you is true love!"

McTavish was about ready to make a beeline towards the front door regardless, until he heard Abby's very audible gasp. He turned towards her to find Abby's face a peculiar shade of crimson as she slowly sunk down on a chair.

"Mom, are you ok?"

Abby was in a no-response mode and Audrey knew that the only time this sort of thing happened was when her mom was sitting on top of some pretty deeply buried emotions. Quickly assessing the situation, Audrey knew she had to act fast.

On the one hand, Abby was clearly incapacitated, to the point that logical conversation was not going to happen. On the other hand, her mom was sharing the living room with a fairly sensitive, reasonably handsome guy who was looking for the same thing that she was, almost hand-picked by fate. Audrey's first thought was: Geez, how cool is that! Her second thought was: If someone doesn't sort this out pronto, Mr. McTavish is going to head for the door, run home, pack his bags and move out of town, right after mom opens her mouth and says something sarcastic like: Good grief Mr. McTavish, some of us never grow up, do we?

While Audrey's brain was working overtime, Abby was having a couple thoughts of her own, like: Why couldn't George Bailey have told Mary that he loved her, point blank, right off the bat? And while we're on the subject, why do men, in general, seem just as emotionally dense nowadays as they did in 1946?

Goodness, thought Abby, I have to step up to the plate real fast here and answer McTavish. But Audrey was already prepared to pitch hit. "Mr. McTavish. If you're looking for true love, you aren't going to find it going door to door. This is America, not the Czech Republic. We don't do things like that around here. If you really want something, you have to get passionate about it, and dropping off computer-generated flyers to strangers just doesn't cut it."

Ordinarily, what Audrey said would have absolutely driven McTavish to jump through their living room window. But instead, he remained seated. And Abby was given just enough time to bypass her fears, take a deep breath, smile and say: "Mr. McTavish, what Audrey means to say is that we'd be delighted to have you as our guest for lunch. That is, if you don't have any plans?"

McTavish, who was smart enough to realize when fate was being kind to him, smiled back at the both of them, graciously accepting their invitation.

Buber

Part of the reason Buber continued to work for Mussfield Auto was that everyone had the same uniform. White slacks, white shirt, no buttons on the collar, and white lab coat. From the backside it was hard to distinguish males from females, let alone individuals. So there was no logical reason to get your fur ruffled over anyone's on-the-job wardrobe.

The only time anyone deviated from the uniform was the annual Halloween tailgate party. Employees were encouraged to dress up as their favorite superhero, within limits of respectability, during their lunch break. Of course, it was totally optional, but about half of the Mussfield associates elected to don a cape or tights or body armor for the occasion. Buber always dressed up as Ready Kilowatt (the cartoon character from the 1950s used by General Electric to encourage families headed up by WWII veterans to spend a good portion of their paychecks on time-saving devices that were guaranteed to add a few dollars to your utility bill).

He lived in a modest neighborhood, a subdivision that had originally been built in the 1950s to house veterans and their spouses. 'Starter homes,' they used to call them, two bedrooms, one bath, small yard, affordable enough while whetting a person's appetite for something bigger. It's ironic, thought Buber, how no one builds those kind of homes anymore. As if a young family can jump into a mortgage payment for a $120,000 home like it's no one's business.

Most Saturday afternoons in the summer Buber could be found outside doing yard work. After five days of being confined to a production line and forced air, it was a joy to feel the breeze on his skin and the warmth of the sun.

It was at times like these that Buber felt that all was right with the world. Being outside, on a sunny day, at the beginning of a Midwestern spring was heaven on earth. That is, until his long-standing next door neighbor passed away and the house was put up for sale. Going on the market during a down economy didn't help matters, and for 16 months, the property sat idle. The only traffic at the house was the yard-person the real estate agent had hired to mow the lawn and trim the shrubbery.

Vita was 40 years old. She had strong arms and calf muscles from being on her feet all day. Her family had come to Texas from Mexico in the 1960s, following the crops up to Michigan. Her father had started out as a migrant worker, saving every penny he could. He had met Vita's mother working in the fields when they were both teenagers. Long before she had caught his eye, Maria had noticed Emilio picking strawberries. She casually moved up to the row next to his, but he hardly noticed her until tomatoes were being harvested.

At first he had accused her of stealing the best rows. But her easy smile and warm eyes quickly convinced him that she had meant no harm.

"I think it's best if we work the row together," she had told him.

"Why?" he had asked.

"Because the work goes faster when you share it and we'll both wind up with more money at the end of the day."

Who could argue with sound logic like that?

She was his match. She could pick right alongside him and even be a step ahead. Theirs was not a case of love at first sight, but more like a friendship that deepened with each lunchtime break.

"What do you think of free love?" he had asked her once, in between bites of an apple.

Maria looked him directly in the eye. "It's a lot like that apple you're eating," she told him. "Why would you pay for the tree when you can keep on getting all the fruit you want for nothing?"

After four years of summertime conversations like that, Emilio asked Maria to meet him at the end of a row that was at the edge of a steep hill. They sat down and as they were watching a spectacular sunset, he asked her to marry him.

"We should get married right away," he told her.

"Why?"

"Because we're good for each other."

Being the more practical of the two, she had told him: "If we're so good for each other, why don't we wait until we have a little more money?"

"There will never be enough money. That's not what makes a marriage. Love makes a marriage. And we have plenty of that."

He was 19 years old. She was 18. They were married in the same field a week later with their family and friends surrounding them. One year later Vita was born.

So, here Vita was, most definitely harboring the combined DNA of her father and mother, maneuvering a mower across the back yard of Buber's former neighbor. As she cut the grass Vita was thinking of a particular birthday celebration, when she was ten years old. Because it was a special celebration, Emilio had gone to the store to get a case of Coke. Normally Maria didn't allow soft drinks in the house. When the rest of the family – two other girls and two boys – heard Emilio's car pull into the driveway, they immediately sprang to the table as Maria pulled out three trays of ice cubes and filled their glasses. The candles on the cake were lit as Emilio passed the Cokes around, each child receiving their own bottle.

Maria was all smiles as she brought the cake into the room, beginning the chorus of "Happy Birthday." Vita's smile was even bigger as she looked at each of her siblings and then at her parents. All of them were smiling back at her. She knew it was a special moment to be in the presence of such love.

"Hey!" Buber shouted.

Vita was still ten years old, soaking in the radiance of that memory, and didn't hear him.

"Excuse me" Buber shouted a bit louder, startling her out of the reminiscence.

She reluctantly turned off the mower and looked at him. "Yes?"

"I was wondering when you're going to be finished up here."

Vita had a very thick skin. In the conflux of the DNA pool between parents, she had inherited an extremely strong work ethic, combined with a genuine love of people. So, instead of tossing back a sarcastic comment to Buber, she took a rag out of her back pocket and wiped her forehead, giving Buber a chance to readjust his attitude a little. Then she smiled, walked over to him and held out her hand. To be sure it was Customer Service 101, but nine times out of ten, this sort of thing worked.

"Hi, I'm Vita Morales."

"I didn't ask what your name was," Buber shot back, ignoring the extended hand.

"No, you didn't. But I always like to know who I'm speaking with, don't you?" Vita was still smiling.

"Most of the time, I don't find that necessary." Couldn't this person put two and two together and figure out she had woken up someone who was working third shift? he thought. What do I have to do, come out here in broad daylight in my pajamas?

"Oh, I find people's names intriguing. I mean, usually our first name was given to remind us of a relative, or friend, or someone or something that's influential." I've got a live one here, thought Vita. But I haven't a clue as to why he's so irritated. Better just go with the flow and see what happens. This go-with-the-flow technique she learned from her father. Emilio had been a master of determining a person's emotional climate. He had taught Vita that most times, when you come across an angry person, the anger isn't meant for you, but you're a lightning rod for someone or something else. The trick is to figure out who or what that something else was, before you were struck.

Buber's eyes narrowed. He was a production supervisor and co-workers knew that when his eyes narrowed, he was about to say something sarcastic to let off a little steam. He was 25 years out of high school, with a tendency to jump to judgment before getting any hard facts. It made for quick decision-making, but left a stream of soured relationships behind. Not that he was one to mind the lack of human companionship. He worked nights, so during the week he was usually asleep when the rest of the world was socializing. And although he had seniority, which meant weekends off, he was getting to the point in the aging process that he needed those days to catch up on his rest.

"Look, I'm not out here to engage you in conversation," he said. He actually held back from what he had wanted to say. It was almost a foreign experience but he was finding Vita's presence to be so inviting that he couldn't help but be influenced by it. "I don't mean anything personal. Just trying to get some sleep."

While Buber was speaking his piece, Vita also detected a change in his attitude. Her mother's DNA was beginning to kick in. "You must work third shift, huh? I'm sorry for the inconvenience."

It was a small observation, but he was genuinely impressed. "How did you know?"

"Because you don't seem like a couch potato and there's sleepy-sand in your eyes."

"Pardon?"

"Sleepy-sand. That's what my mother used to call the stuff that gets in your eyes when you've slept overnight."

Despite himself, he laughed out loud.

"You find that funny?"

"No, I mean yes. I've never heard it called that before. It's like you're sharing a family secret."

"Actually, I am."

It was Buber who was beginning to get intrigued now. "Why would you choose to do that? We're strangers."

"Well, that's not totally the case now, is it? I know that you're a neighbor of whoever owns this lot."

"Casey's dead. It's not rocket science. Past owner dies, family that inherits the property doesn't want it, but they want to sell, so they keep it maintained."

So that's where the lightning comes from, she thought. Vita paused a moment to lightly touch Buber's arm. "I'm so sorry for your loss. Were you close?"

(What do you choose to tell about a deep friendship? What do you keep secret up front to protect the memories? How far do you trust someone with something so emotionally precious while you're in the awkward process of getting to know each other?)

"You have no idea."

"I'd like to," was all she said, extending an invitation to continue the conversation.

In that instant Buber felt something inside him shift. "Casey McVeigh. That was his full name. He was third generation Irish."

He told Vita how Casey's great-grandfather came over from County Donegal because of the potato famine. The two older children stayed behind and eventually headed to Belfast to work in the shipping yards. They never saw their family again. Two of six kids who came on the boat with their parents were buried at sea. Another one died on Ellis Island. His great-granddad didn't have time to grieve. He had a wife and three kids to take care of, so they headed to Brooklyn. They lived in a tenement. He worked as a laborer and saved his money. A few years later they got out of New York and moved out to Michigan and bought some land. They were farmers. Casey was the first in his family to break loose from the soil.

"Casey got himself a good paying factory job. In the same plant where I've been working since high school." Buber paused, feeling a little embarrassed for having revealed so much information.

Intuitively Vita knew to ask the next question. "How did your dad feel about your working in a factory so young?"

"My dad wasn't around to think much about it. He left my mom when I was in grade school and we never heard from him after that. We struggled to put food on the table and I saw the toll she paid for not earning enough. Casey was a great role model and he encouraged me. The work was hard but they paid you very well. Once I signed on, I knew my mom would never have to worry about finances again."

"But you're obviously smart. I mean, did you ever think about college?"

Vita was smart too. In fact, her parents had placed a big emphasis on getting a good education. From first grade on they would scrutinize her report card and ask follow up questions about any class where she didn't get an "A." Fortunately, since the hour before dinner and at least an hour after clean-up were devoted to studying, she very seldom had conversations about her grades. She was encouraged to apply for scholarships to college, and she even received a few offers. One included the University of Michigan. But when she saw the cost of tuition and room and board, it quickly became apparent that there wasn't enough money to go around for her other siblings. So, she deferred to them, went to a community college for two years, continued to get straight "A"s and left it at that. Besides, the landscaping firm she worked for had given her a partnership. It was a small company but it was growing.

"All the monkeys aren't in the zoo," Buber said.

She laughed. "Meaning all smart people don't necessarily attend college?"

"There are different kinds of smart."

Who was this guy? She thought. He works in a factory but he doesn't talk like a factory worker at all.

"So, were you academically inclined?"

Buber raised his eyebrows. "No, if you mean, did I get good grades. My focus wasn't on school-based learning. But I was one of those kids who hung out at the library. Every chance I got, in between working, I'd have my nose in a book."

"What kinds of books?"

"Philosophy. Theology. Sociology, mostly, that sort of thing." He shrugged. "No one was teaching those subjects in middle school."

Vita's parents had been raised Mexican Catholic. The kind that made do with five o'clock masses on Saturdays with guitar worship in Spanish. Emilio and Maria had grown up with the Charismatic Renewal of the late 1960s, so by the time Vita was born they were heavily influenced by its freedom towards the Holy Spirit. Which eventually led them to join a storefront Iglesia on the fringes of the inner city.

It was into this small but determined bunch of believers that Vita was born. Her earliest memories of church included Sunday services that consisted of an hour of pre-service prayer, an hour of worship and an hour of preaching. She grew up on heart-felt worship with a band that included a trumpet, saxophone and stand up bass.

Buber, on the other hand, was raised by an agnostic mother who distrusted men too much to leave her soul in the hands of one. This was somewhat offset by Casey's influence, whose family had kept their Irish Catholic roots intact, handing Casey a rich tradition as fragrant as the incense used at High Mass on feast days.

Although Buber was attracted to the rich liturgical customs of Catholicism, his longing was more for the inward transformation rather than the outward sign of any sacrament.

"So, you're the designated professor of the production line then?" Vita said.

"Not exactly. You have to have an audience to be a professor, and most lunch hours I pull a book out of my locker and read, off in a corner table out of sight. I'm not much for social interaction in the workplace, outside of team meetings. How about yourself?"

"I always carry a paperback in my lunchbox as a back-up, but I've had some amazing conversations with the associates I've worked with."

"Such as?"

"Well, we tend to get the younger crowd home on college break earning money during the summer. I love to hear what they're thinking. It amazes me how they seem to want something to commit to, outside of work. The corporate world just doesn't hack it with them anymore."

Buber agreed. "Yeah. We get college kids in during the summer too, and the times I've been roped into sitting at a lunch table with them, I have to admit they are earnestly fed up with money as the primary motivator for a career choice."

"Kind of reminds you of the 60s, doesn't it? I mean, from what our parents told us of it? The days of the Weathermen and the SDS and Caesar Chavez, Abbie Hoffman and the Pentagon Papers."

Vita nodded before changing the subject. "So, am I correct in assuming that you're not much of a joiner?"

"That would be a fair assumption."

"Does that include church services?"

"Pretty much, yes. Why do you ask?"

There was a gleam in her eyes now. "I'm not one for joining anything for joining's sake either," she said "But there's something about getting together with a group of folks who are seeking the Lord."

Buber had been around the proverbial block a few times, but he had never heard the motivation for attending church services phrased that way. For her part, Vita too had taken a number of circulatory trips around a different mountain. Remembering her own frustration of that spent time, she recognized the source of Buber's lack of social skills. She had received the grace to submit to the emotional surgery required to forgive and leave the past behind. In Vita's case it was the need to forgive peers throughout her childhood who had openly displayed prejudice of another race and of others living in poverty. It had been the most difficult period of her young life, but on the other side came an overwhelming and now natural inclination to display love rather than judgment towards others.

"What do you mean?" Buber's response elicited nothing but empathy.

"Getting together with others who love God is so essential for me. Those times are the high points of my week."

Buber instinctively raised his eyebrows. "You're serious?"

"Absolutely! You should come to my church sometime."

There was something in the tone of Vita's voice that was genuine. It was enough to lift Buber out of his usual social funk. She isn't a holy roller-type at all, he thought. She wasn't preaching to him; in fact, her natural way of talking about spiritual things was intriguing. So, despite his past experience, he found that Vita was drawing out a side of him that had been lying dormant for a long time.

"Sure, yeah, I mean I don't work on weekends. How about this Sunday?" Buber said.

Vita's smile couldn't have been wider.

Carmello & Gilda: A Christmas Story

Carmello was minding his own business, sitting down off the beaten path, a half mile away from the 72nd Street entrance to Central Park on the West Side. He worked at the Eddie Bauer outlet on Columbus Avenue and since it was an unusually warm day in early December, he had spontaneously decided to spend his lunch hour soaking in the sun.

The weeks right after Thanksgiving were always the busiest at the store, and this shopping season had been a tough one. Despite reports of a down economy, you'd never be able to guess it by the store's traffic. Anyway Carmello was no economist, and he was looking forward to a few precious minutes of peace and quiet. He slowly closed his eyes and began to relax.

"Excuse me," came the soft, feminine voice.

Determined to stay in a state of comfort, Carmello kept his eyes shut while responding. "Yes?"

"Can I bother you for a second?"

He slowly nodded yes.

"I'm really sorry, but I'm good and lost."

Realizing this wasn't a native New Yorker talking, or if it were, it was one who was creative enough to come up with a pretty good pick-up line, he opened his eyes.

She was standing right in front of him, smiling, another sure sign she wasn't a native. "I'm so sorry, but I have absolutely no idea where I am. I mean, I know this is Central Park, but I sort of wandered in after crossing Fifth Avenue a while back."

"So, where are you headed?" he asked.

"That's the problem, for sure!" she answered back. "I can't seem to make up my mind. I mean, I was hired to do production, but they've got me doing marketing. Which in itself isn't all bad, but the thing of it is, I suck at marketing. My degree is in English, so it's a stretch as it is. I've been pretty loyal for the past year with this situation, but I'm just about fed up. But then I think, hey, most people would give their right eye to be here."

"You said you were lost, so I was asking where were you trying to go?" Carmello said.

"That's what I'm trying to tell you," she answered. "Do you mind if I sit down, I'm not exactly wearing walking shoes."

"Yeah, sure. It's a public park, be my guest."

Carmello was not the sort of person who went out of his way to meet new people. He was a Midwestern transplant and didn't have the gift of gab.

"I was supposed to go on an interview at ABC this afternoon. That's where I was headed, but then I thought, you know, it's way too nice a day to hail a taxi, I'm going to foot it. So, I walked into Central Park and then next thing I know, here I am."

He was thinking: You have got to be kidding. You've been living in the City for heaven knows how long and you still don't know your way around the Park? But what came out of his mouth was: "Yeah, it's easy to get lost. Used to happen to me all the time when I first moved here."

Why was he offering this woman a tidbit of information that he hadn't told anyone in the seven years he had lived in Manhattan? It wasn't that he was divulging something secret, but to someone like Carmello, sharing even this little piece of his past was an act of intimacy.

"You know, I really don't feel comfortable interviewing for this associate producer's position. I mean, technically, it's a type of internship that's supposed to lead to an inside track for advancement. But do I really care about learning how to put window dressing on the nightly news?"

Carmello only shrugged in response.

"Could you just give me a second? I have to make a call." Carmello shrugged again, this time while lifting his eyebrows in an act of resignation, while she made her call to ABC to let them know she was bailing out on the interview. It took all of twenty seconds.

"Thanks! You've been extremely helpful," she said.

"No problem."

"I'm Gilda, by the way," she said extending her hand for a good, old-fashioned hand shake. "Gilda Rudner. Pleased to make your acquaintance."

Gilda was named for her grandmother, who had come to the United States from Russia at the turn of the 19th Century. She became an atheist after all the Jews were run out of their village, figuring, "if this is what living Kosher gets you, I'm no longer interested." Eventually Gilda's grandmother met Levi Roth, who had been forced to leave another Russian village. They married and had one child, Morgan, the younger Gilda's mother.

Fast forward to the younger Gilda, who grew up in Riverdale, which was interesting because even though Riverdale is a hop and a skip from Manhattan, she hadn't been to the City until she moved there for a job two years ago. So, here she was, a native of the Bronx who knew next to nothing about Manhattan, asking a dyed-in-the-wool transplant for directions.

What could he do now? He felt obligated to accept her handshake. "Carmello Bartuchi. And I have to say, I mean, this probably is obvious, but you aren't from around here, are you?"

Gilda let out a laugh that caused a few nearby squirrels to go scampering. "Actually, I am! Born and raised in the Bronx, Riverdale to be exact. We non-practicing Jews don't get out a lot."

"Pardon?" To be honest, Carmello had been staring at Gilda's jet black hair and was noticing the way it perfectly matched her black eyes. He found it to be alarmingly beautiful.

"I just told you, I'm Jewish, from Riverdale, but I've never been to synagogue."

"Oh."

"But you're right. I definitely don't know my way around the nooks and crannies of this city at all. I must be the only native who doesn't call Manhattan 'The City.' I mean, how pretentious is that anyway? To refer to this place like that? As if this were the end of the line."

Carmello was from Michigan. When he was 26 he had packed everything he could stuff inside a backpack, including a frying pan and a corduroy jacket for job interviews and took the Amtrak to New York. Carmello's sense of responsibility led him to feel that if he wasn't job hunting he should be studying, so for the first six months after he set foot in Manhattan he spent every Saturday inside the main branch of the Public Library on Fifth and 42nd Street. Typically he'd request three or four books, reading through them while taking notes. After a few hours, he'd take a break and get something to eat. It never ceased to amaze him how shocked he continued to be each time he opened the library door and walked down the steps into the hubbub of Midtown. It was so foreign to him that he might as well have been in Singapore.

"So, what's your story? I mean, you've got the out-of-town accent, but you could be from anywhere."

"I'm from Battle Creek, Michigan. About halfway between Detroit and Chicago."

"You have got to be joking!" now she was the one raising her eyebrows in disbelief. "My parents had relatives in South Haven. We rented a cottage right across the street from the Lake! I loved it! What great summers we had, swimming and walking along the beach! Those were some of the most relaxing times of my life! Wow! What are the chances that a person would go for a walk in Central Park, get totally lost and wind up asking someone from the Great Lake State for directions!"

She had vivid memories of her dad rustling up driftwood, fuel for early-evening clam bakes that stretched on into the evening. The taste of the garlic butter sauce spread on the seafood, corn on the cob, and fresh bread; and when you were completely stuffed, lying on your back, eagerly pointing out shooting stars in the early August sky. The laughter of her Dad and Mom like a magic elixir, blending with the ebb and flow of the waves lapping against the shore. This was the epitome of satisfaction.

Wouldn't you know it – Carmello had never set foot on Lake Michigan's shore? His family didn't have a car until he was in junior high school. His father came from a long line of high energy Sicilians, but his mother was the complete opposite, having grown up in a sleepy river boat town at the tip of southern Illinois.

"I've actually never been to Lake Michigan," he told her.

Gilda was instantly compassionate. "What a shame! Living so close to it."

Carmello was ready to change the subject. "You must have gone to Wave Hill then, being from Riverdale?"

"No. My favorite Riverdale thing to do was walk to Riverdale Park and stare out at the Palisades. When I was young, I used to imagine what it must have been like for Henry Hudson to sail down that gorgeous river for the first time. I thought, it had to be during the fall when the trees have their peak color, reflected in the river. Floating on a liquid sea of yellows and reds and golds. Everyone on that ship with him must have felt they had died and sailed to heaven!"

This was Gilda at her best. Utterly under the influence of her imagination. Immersed in her senses. Completely oblivious to time and living in a city that did not suffer romantics lightly.

"So, have you had lunch yet?" Gilda offered. It was her turn to shrug her shoulders. "It's totally fine if you already have. You've probably already eaten right? I mean, it's called the lunch hour, not the lunch afternoon. It's the middle of the busiest shopping season of the year; you're lucky you had a chance to get out at all. Or maybe you were just sitting here soaking up the sun waiting for your sweetheart to show up?"

It was Carmello's turn to laugh. What was it with this woman? And why was he finding her so attractive? Did she catch him in between a power-snooze and a dream? "No," was all he could manage.

"No to what?" she shot back. "No to lunch, the shopping season, or your sweetheart?"

It really wasn't Gilda's fault. She had grown up with two older brothers, and between them they had taught her how to be a real smarty-pants. Luckily for her sake, her mother's sweetness softened the natural inclination to verbally spar, so she was never obnoxious or mean. Just quick on the draw to keep the conversation flowing. Much like the conversations she was accustomed to over the family dinner table. Tempered with references to Buber and Bonhoeffer, with a little of Bob Hope thrown in for good measure. She was no philosophical slouch.

"No to all of that, I guess," said Carmello. Unlike Gilda, he was a little slower to formulate a response. But it wasn't due to lack of ability. Actually it was quite the opposite. Normally his brain offered too many options to choose from and he enjoyed considering each of them, typically Midwestern in his inclination to wait for the bud to blossom before picking it.

"Well, what do you say that we take advantage of the hot dog stand that eagerly awaits our business?" she said, motioning with her eyes.

"But you can't eat pork, can you?"

"It's ok. Don't you know that the hot dog guys in Manhattan only sell kosher dogs?"

"Really?"

"I have no idea. Like I said, we didn't practice; I've never set foot in a synagogue, and aren't you hungry?"

"Yes, sure."

She had two with ketchup, mustard, onions and relish. He had two with sauerkraut heaped on them.

"Wow, you must have some German in your blood from somewhere!"

"As a matter of fact, I don't. My grandparents on my mother's side were French and first generation in this country."

"Mine were strictly Russian, both sides. But from different towns."

As they were eating they talked about schooling. She had gone to Manhattan College, not that far from where she grew up. He had gone to Hope College in his home state. She told him about the difference between the Torah and the Talmud. He mentioned purgatory and original sin, which she didn't seem to find very original.

"When it comes down to it, aren't most people still interested in biting off more than they can chew? I mean, what was the attraction of being like God if you took a bite of forbidden fruit? Adam must have had a monstrous ego."

"Why would you say that?"

"Because Eve was tricked, flat out, but Adam very easily could have passed on a nibble. Couldn't he have seen it was a sham by looking into his wife's eyes, for heaven's sake?"

"I never thought about it that way."

"Of course you never. You're not a woman!"

One thing they both had in common was transference of religious guilt.

"For Jews, it's part of our ethnic makeup. If we don't leave the house in the morning with fifty different things to feel guilty about, we feel naked."

"As a kid, I felt guilty for not having enough sins to confess. Then as an adult I'd feel guilty about not going to confession at all."

"Did you reach a resolution?"

"When the Church made the move to general absolution, it helped out a lot."

"Yom Kippur does it for us."

Carmello hadn't had this much lunch hour fun since the time the store closed four hours early when the building's boiler unit conked out. There really wasn't an alternative to letting the sales associates go home early because it was late fall and the store quickly became too cold to shop in. Not a fun experience in itself, but it became fun because he suddenly had paid free time in the middle of the work day.

He wound up walking to the Public Library's Lincoln Center branch that afternoon, checking out a biography of James Agee, who may have been the most hard-working alcoholic writer in America for his time period.

Carmello thought: What is it with these suffering artists anyway? Why can't they just learn to forgive and forget? That question would have to go unanswered as Gilda had one of her own.

"So what do you think?"

Carmello arched his eyebrows.

"I'm having a great time, sitting here eating a hot dog with you." As if to prove her point, she smiled – extraordinarily heartfelt but shyly.

This girl has guts, thought Carmello.

Gilda was thinking: The big-city approach would be to say something slightly sarcastic, or else pretend like this was just one of those chance encounters you used to read about in the New Yorker. But the truth is, I'm beginning to like this guy and I'd feel awful if I never saw him again. I mean, there has got to be a reason that we met up today. Or do people go around striking up conversations like this 24/7? The worst things in the world are unspoken feelings.

What she said was: "Untaken chances really, really suck."

Carmello smiled back, but waited to respond. He could tell that Gilda had more on her mind.

"Is it big-city life, or just being human? I mean, would it be any easier for us to have a conversation if we were a couple of farmers in Iowa or someplace like that? Out in the middle of a cornfield moseying along? I'm probably talking too much," she said. "Well, that and over-thinking."

Carmello took Gilda's empty food container. "I was born anxious, it wouldn't have mattered one bit where I grew up."

In truth, Gilda had been a bit of a goody two-shoes, but not purposely. She couldn't help getting straight A's in school and earning a full ride to Manhattan College. So what if it was a Catholic institution? The education was top-notch and it didn't hurt to get the inside scoop on the mother of Jesus, did it? Gilda came to love the option of daily Mass. Attracted to the symbolism and tradition of it, she found it a great way to start the morning. Although she had to opt out of receiving communion, she was attracted to the possibility of having the Eucharistic celebration centered around something, that from a distance, looked suspiciously like matzos.

Growing up it had been a little unnerving to see neighbors walking to the synagogue every Sabbath, wondering what it was like. Whenever she asked her parents about it, they told her that some Jews had a special way of approaching the Eternal One, but, from what they could tell, the Eternal One didn't seem to play favorites.

"My parents didn't have much in common except sexual attraction when they first met," said Carmello. "But they could both cook up a storm, so we had magnificent meals. It's hard to beat fettuccini alfredo with crepe suzettes for dessert. Our saving grace was the Mediterranean Diet. Fruits and vegetables brought us together."

"I am so jealous! If you ever want to know the benefits of borscht, I'm your gal."

It was now Carmello's turn to let out a belly laugh.

"So, what exactly is borscht anyway?"

"Beets are the essential ingredient. If you want to know more, it'll cost you a dinner."

Carmello was thinking: I would have settled for a lunch. But dinner is fine, great, actually. Gilda was thinking, wow, who knew I had such chutzpah? I must really like this guy.

"Sure. Dinner would be nice. I live on West 72nd, off of West End Avenue. But we could meet near your place." Normally he wasn't so definitive, but it was a nice gesture that Gilda appreciated.

"I'm on Lexington, near 76th. Want to meet in the lobby of Lenox Hill Hospital and eat in their cafeteria?"

Carmello only arched his eyebrows at that one.

"Just kidding! Really, who would do a thing like that? I mean, unless we were a couple of surgeons. Hand me your cell phone."

Under normal circumstances, Carmello wouldn't turn over his cell to anyone. But his instincts told him to trust this woman who had the ability to make him forget the rush of the holiday season. So, he followed Gilda's lead. It only took a few seconds for her to punch in her phone number.

"There. You've got it." She handed over her cell to him. "Now when you give me yours, we'll be set."

"How does tonight sound?" asked Carmello, who couldn't believe that he was smiling so broadly.

"Well, seeing how it's not Sabbath, it should be fine," she said. "Really, that's very sweet to agree to have dinner with a non-Kosher stranger from Riverdale."

Carmello had a hunch that they wouldn't be strangers for long.

Eyre Square

Jon was on the 'magic bus' headed towards Galway with the outreach team, such as it was. Kevin was at the wheel, in a great mood, as usual.

Of course he is, thought Jon. He lives for this sort of thing. The other members of the motley crew were Devin, suffering from severe depression, who had been given a weekend pass from a mental institution; Trevor, who was engaged to Suzanne, a gorgeous Scot; and Renzor, who was built like a stick, with a wicked sense of humor, and played the guitar, so he was the team's musical director, by default.

The trip itself was fairly unremarkable. With the exception of stopping to pick up a young hitchhiker. Kevin opened up the bus door (the 'magic bus' was actually a full-size bus that had been converted for missionary work by ripping out the back half of the seats and installing a makeshift kitchenette with shelves and a hot plate which ran on propane).

"Welcome!" said Kevin. Before 'giving his life over to Jesus,' Kevin had been involved with the IRA, to the point of having been capped, in an attempt to scare him into squealing on his friends. Capping was used by both sides and involved holding a pistol next to a person's kneecap and then pulling the trigger. It resulted in intense pain and partial paralysis. On a few occasions Kevin had been kidnapped from his bed in the middle of the night, pillowcase pulled over his head, and taken to a remote place far out of town, where he was beaten, stripped and threatened.

The hitchhiker took one look inside the bus and smiled. "Are you guys out for a bit of fun?"

"Oh yes," answered Kevin. "It's always that way when we're on the road telling people about the most wonderful person who ever lived!"

"And who would that be?"

"Jesus," said Devin. "He's the most wonderful. Now and forever."

Kevin and Jon had visited Devin several times during his most recent bout, and hadn't been successful to get him to say one word, not alone an entire sentence. So to keep the conversation going, Kevin had stuck to asking Devin questions that he could answer with a simple nod of his head. When Kevin had mentioned that he wanted Devin to be part of his outreach crew, Jon had balked.

"Are you sure? I mean, the man is seriously under it. How on earth is he going to engage other people if he can't even engage his own self?"

"Reaching out to others is a perfect way to get Devin out of his shell," said Kevin.

"Yeah, maybe under normal circumstances. But you saw the man. He's just not in a place to communicate."

"Then we'll trust God to open his mouth, won't we?"

As far as Kevin was concerned, it was a done deal. Being the only non-Irish person on the team, Jon knew better than to second guess a native. Besides, he had high regard for the strong sense of spirituality that was part of the Irish heritage, even if it was that same strong sense that the devil had twisted to tangle up the country in The Troubles.

So the hitchhiker sat down next to Devin, who turned to Renzor.

"Can I see your guitar?" Devon asked.

Renzor nodded, handing it over.

Devin began to strum the chords to "Amazing Grace" and then to sing. His voice filled the bus up with its sweetness, soon joined by Renzor's harmony. By the time they sang the last verse, the hitchhiker was crying softly. He looked at Devin.

"Thank you," he said.

"No problem," said Devin, as he handed the guitar back to its owner.

"That was lovely. I haven't really thought about God in a while," said the hitchhiker. "I guess I needed to be reminded."

"We all do."

Right before getting into Galway, the hitchhiker asked to be let out.

It was around half past six when the 'magic bus' pulled into Eyre Square for the night. Kevin sent Jon and Renzor out to get fish and chips while Devin and Kevin put on some tea. After eating, Kevin spoke up.

"So, today was finals at the University. Kids are going to be crossing the Square on their way back and forth from the pubs. We're here to offer an ear, some biscuits, and a non-alcoholic alternative. And to offer a place to chat about whatever's on their minds."

And this is what made Jon nervous. He was an American and not used to something so spontaneous. Maybe that's why it was easier for the Irish to be spiritually minded. Their general outlook was not pinned to the bottom line, so they could relax and enjoy the trip along the way.

The team spent some time praying and then waiting to see who would show up. The first person to come on the bus wasn't a student. She was a woman in her early 30s, on her way to drowning her sorrows. Kevin looked at Jon, saw how nervous he was, and immediately motioned Jon to pour her some tea.

"Thanks," she said, taking the cup like it was a chalice. "My name's Mary Beth."

"Pleased to meet you," Jon answered.

"Have any sugar?

Jon handed her a few packets of sugar. She asked for a few more.

"I like it sweet."

Jon nodded, noticing her American accent.

"I'm stuck," she sighed. "I came here ten years ago. A week after I got here, I met the most delicious looking Irishman. Blue eyes, thick curly black hair. The lilt of his voice was mesmerizing. So when he asked me to marry him, I did. From that point forward my life became a dream. Rorick and I spent more time in bed that out of it. I had never experienced anything like that. Ever.

Mary Beth's hands began to tremble as she continued.

"Slowly my man got a hold on me. Then a blackness settled in. I could never do anything right, the way he wanted it. And I couldn't go out of the house without his approval. It was like a noose was hanging around my neck, getting tighter all the time. Then he began to hit me. At first he'd apologize. Even act remorseful about it. But eventually, the apologies were replaced by threats. I had to switch off my mind to cope with it. I became dead to myself.

"But one morning, I was hunched over the stove, cooking his breakfast. He was in a particularly foul mood, yelling, calling me stupid because I couldn't seem to boil an egg to his liking. He walked over and when he raised his hand to hit me, something snapped inside. I picked up the iron skillet I was going to use to fry bacon and hit him hard as I could on the head.

"He passed out on the floor, blood oozing from his mouth, so I very calmly picked up the phone and called an ambulance. By the time the paramedics got to our flat, he was dead. When the police came, they checked with neighbors who verified that they had heard us arguing pretty consistently. And it turned out that Rorick had a history of domestic abuse. That day I was set free from him, but the pain continued."

Jon poured Mary Beth another cup of tea. "How so?"

"Rorick's death didn't stop the intense hate. So I began

drinking. Because I have Irish ancestry and had married an Irishman, I was automatically good to stay in the country, but I might as well have been on the moon. I mean, this place has become an absolute nightmare to me.

Jon put a few biscuits on a plate and set them before Mary Beth. "Please, go on."

"I drink because I'm so angry. For two straight years now, it's what I have to do to get through the day. One thing has led to another and I found myself in Galway, paying the rent and getting my drinking money by turning tricks with students who are out to get their first sexual experience. Sort of ironic, isn't it? I mean, here are these wet-behind-the-ears puppy-dogs who are looking for love. They get their heads all full of Keats and Byron and Shelley and the next thing you know they're in a pub on the make. Because I'm American, it's an added turn-on to them."

"But that's not really love."

"Who said it was?" Mary Beth laughed at the assumption.

At this point Devin picked up Renzor's guitar and started strumming. He sat there playing so gently that the music had the effect of bringing a calm to Mary Beth's spirit.

"God loves you," he said.

Mary Beth turned towards him. "How can you say that? How can you know that?"

"Because he sent his son to die for you."

"But I'm so messed up. Really, really messed up. I've taken away the virginity of more young men that I can count. And you'd be surprised how many of them tell me they love me right after they pay me."

"God loves you," he repeated.

"Some of them even want to spend the night with me. But I tell them all to go back home and forget about me. That's a solid rule I've had from the very beginning, to keep emotional attachment out of it."

"God loves you," Devin said for the third time as he picked the guitar back up and kept playing.

Slowly, at first, Mary Beth began crying, then the tears came faster and thicker, trickling down her cheeks. Jon awkwardly offered her a box of tissues.

"Thanks for the tea," she said softly.

"You're welcome."

"And thank you for listening."

"No problem," said Jon, offering a genuine smile.

And that's the way it seemed to go the entire night, with a lull every now and then, until about three in the morning. Things were quieting down, when a young man crossing the Square walked onto the bus.

"So, what's this all about?" he said.

"Would you like a cup of tea?" asked Jon.

Trevor explained the concept of using the bus to minister God's love to others. The young man's name was James, and he explained that he had just finished leaving a pub, engrossed with a group of friends talking about their various girlfriends and boyfriends and how they each fell short.

"Why do you even bother?" James asked.

"Bother?"

"Trying to show love. It doesn't exist. At least not in its truest form."

"Maybe we could start by defining it," said Trevor, who reached for his Bible, turning to the 13th chapter of the first book of Corinthians. "Tell me what you think of this: 'Love suffers long and is kind; love does not envy; love does not parade itself, is not puffed up; does not behave rudely, does not seek its own, is not provoked, thinks no evil; does not rejoice in iniquity, but rejoices in the truth; bears all things, believes all things, hopes all things, endures all things. Love never fails.'"

"Do you actually know anyone who loves like that? I mean, I've searched my whole life for love, but it hasn't worked out. I keep getting burned and it's wearing me out. If God is love and what you just read is true, then why on earth is it so hard to find?

Or is this some sort of cosmic joke that we experience on earth that we should accept and get on with it?"

"God doesn't play games," said Trevor. He pulled out his wallet and showed James a picture of Suzanne, his fiancée. "She's a gift from God and an expression of his love."

James took a sip of tea. "Yeah, I can see how it's easy for you to rattle on about love, with a gorgeous girl like that!"

"Yes, she's beautiful, but that's not the point."

"So you're saying that you've somehow transcended the physical realm where the eternally abstract supersedes the material?"

"The eternal isn't abstract."

"You know those bumper stickers that say 'Love Wins.' Tell me that's not abstract. Or else please explain how it'll be fulfilled in our lifetime. People have been waiting since creation to see that one come true!"

"The fact that there's a yearning speaks to its existence."

"You can't argue that way. It isn't philosophically solid."

"No it's not, because love is a spiritual principle."

"Which has never been proven!"

"Lots of things have never been proven. That doesn't mean they don't exist."

"Help me understand, then." There was a pleading in James' eyes.

"Can I go back to Corinthians?"

"If you want to."

"Would you agree that the writer of Corinthians had to have some sort of knowledge of love to write so confidently about it?"

"Sure, ok. I can give you that."

"So then, the question becomes where did Paul, the author of that epistle, get his knowledge? Can we agree that's the real question?"

James sat straight up, fully engaged in the conversation. "You mean, what was the source of love that Paul had experienced?"

Trevor nodded his head.

"I haven't a clue!"

"Where do most of us seek love?" Devin spoke up now.

"Family... friends... causes... sex. I don't know, I guess it's a different combination for everyone. Just like my friends and I were talking about earlier tonight. But we had all hit a dead end. None of us could say that we had found complete fulfillment in any type of love that we had experienced. Not a single one. That's why I had to get up and leave. I couldn't stand to think that I'd never find true love. I mean, they were basically telling me to grow up and realize that it doesn't exist."

"But?"

"But I actually believe that it does. Even though I've yet to find it. Otherwise, why would I be longing to experience it?"

"We tend to look for love in the wrong places," said Devin. "But only one being has its truest form."

"Are you going to go God on me now?" he asked.

"Where else haven't you looked?"

"Believe me, I've looked there and he's been found sadly wanting. There's a lion's share of nastiness among followers of religion, in my experience," James said. "If true love really existed among that crowd, don't you think the whole world would have been converted by now?"

"A bit disappointing to find hypocrisy there, is it?" said Jon, re-entering the conversation.

"It's not a safe harbor."

"So, taking your line of logic then, should we dismiss all of the arts because some artists were scoundrels?"

"That's not a valid argument at all," said James. "Artists are humans and we don't worship them. And they never pretend to have a solution for life's dilemmas."

"Isn't it interesting that in one of John's epistles, he writes that one of the chief characteristics of followers of Christ is that they love each other. Actually, he says that God is love. The book of Acts has several references to how the early followers took care of each other."

"What does that prove? Doesn't the Bible also say that it's not a big deal to love someone who loves you back? The truer test is to love the unlovable."

"I think we need to go back to first Corinthians again," said Jon. "Just because people fall short of the ideal, doesn't mean that the ideal doesn't exist."

Jon's heart was beating fast. He wanted to offer encouragement to James, who seemed at his wit's end.

What is it about the Irish, Jon thought? Why are they so prone to latch on to the ironies of life to the exclusion of ultimate truth? Maybe it's because they've been invaded, taken advantage of in every way possible, forced to watch their neighbors starve to death by the millions as their mother country shipped food away to other countries for profit. Not to mention the centuries-old bickering among the Irish themselves – Catholic against Protestant, which was particularly ugly when you thought about all the thousands of people who had been killed.

As if reading his mind, Devin spoke up. "The ultimate reality is that God is love. And God, being love in its purest form, never fails. The perfect expression of God the Father is Jesus. I believe that. I have faith in that."

James looked straight at Devin. "So, from your point of view, true love is linked to God, so it becomes, by default, linked to faith."

"And that's why love never fails!" Devin's face was absolutely radiant with confidence.

James stood up and stretched. For the first time, a smile slowly came across his face. He shook Devin's hand, said "thank you," and walked off the bus into the very early Galway morning.

Ambercrombie

You can tell a lot about a person just by taking a good look at the things they have attached to their refrigerator door. The magnets – some are cute, some are philosophical, some are flat out sarcastic, and some are even the educational type (the ones with random words that force you to create phrases).

And then there's the never-ending series of kids' drawings taped up to fill in the blank space. They don't have to be done by your kids; nieces and nephews work just as well, and in a pinch, so do kids of co-workers. Not to mention flyers of events that happened years ago, and "to do" lists. This one, in itself, is a dead give-away. Be careful about getting involved with someone who actually uses one of those "to do" lists, especially if they have more than ten items written down, and they are very specific. (Not "go grocery shopping," but "get cabernet, goat's cheese and garlic lover's hummus.")

Somewhere in the middle of all of this clutter is guaranteed to be photographs – of a couple smiling at the beach, a group of happy people gathered round a restaurant table, or a prized pet.

If you're lucky you'll find ticket stubs from some cultural event, like the opera, or symphony, or a Broadway show on tour. A dead give away as to artistic preferences, without ever having to ask.

But the interesting thing about Ambercrombie was that her refrigerator door had nothing on it. No magnets, no pictures, no photos, no clever word games, or "to do" lists or ticket stubs. It was clean and bare. Absent of any clues whatsoever as to what was going on in the life of its owner.

What's a clue anyway? Something that points to a possibility?

Ambercrombie was running a little late for work at the publishing house where she was an editor's assistant. It was housed on the 14th floor of a downtown building that had two elevators. No one else was in the lobby, so when she punched "14" once the doors closed she was looking forward to a short, solo flight up. When she heard the automatic ding before the doors opened on 8, she sighed, deeply disappointed. "That's good for another 20 seconds," she thought when the door opened up.

How was Lou Nickels supposed to know what was going on when he stepped inside the elevator to find an intelligent but bothered-looking woman on board? Doesn't hurt to start up a conversation, he thought.

"Morning."

Ambercrombie looked straight ahead.

"Nice day isn't it?"

There was continued silence from her.

"I guess this is the part where you could choose to acknowledge that there's someone else in the elevator with you. Technically, it's only the two of us, but what the heck? I see we're both going to the 14th floor. How's that for a brilliant conversation starter?"

She couldn't help but laugh. "I'm sorry. I work for Fairway Publications and they don't look kindly upon editorial assistants who are late. It's making me a little uptight."

"Pretty cutthroat trying to juggle all those production schedules, eh?"

"Are you in publishing?"

"No, I'm just dropping off some of my photos for a book they're working on."

"That wouldn't be the travel guide for Ireland?"

"One and the same! Supposed to meet with Brenda Hamilton to square some things away before we progress any further."

She held out her hand. "I'm Brenda's assistant, Ambercrombie."

Just then the elevator door opened up. Most of the 14th floor was rented by the Fairway Publications Group, specializing in travel guides and airline magazines.

Lou followed Ambercrombie to Brenda's office, but as the two rounded the corner, she was handed a note which read: *Brenda sick, cover nine o'clock with photo-guy re. Ireland. Use her office.*

So Ambercrombie opened up the door, motioning for Lou to sit down.

"I'm sorry that Brenda can't make it, but she left a message, asking me to take a look at what you've come up with. I'm working with her on the copy, so I've got a good idea of the subject matter."

"Why don't we just use the table so I can spread out the pictures?"

For nearly 20 minutes Lou showed Ambercrombie his work, consisting of shots taken in Belfast, Derry and out-of-the-way places like Crossmaglen and Omagh. The whole idea of the guide was to highlight Northern Ireland and bypass the traditional focus on Dublin and the South (better known as the Republic of Ireland).

"These are good. Really good."

Her assessment caused Lou to smile. "Thanks."

Although Ambercrombie's refrigerator door held no clues, she did have a monstrous chalkboard in her bedroom. In fact it took up almost an entire wall. On one small corner were taped photos of places that she had been, or wanted to go; most of the board was devoted to a listing of churches she was planning on attending, with a scorecard of the ones she had already visited.

The vertical columns were headed: "worship," "teaching," "small groups," "friendliness," and "snacks." Under each, for the scored churches, she had written A, B, C, D or U (U standing for uninteresting).

The reason for the classification system was that Ambercrombie had a few rather unfortunate experiences with organized religion already. She grew up with parents who didn't rule out the existence of God, but had decided not to actively pursue the possibility. So from the time that Ambercrombie and her brother Jason were able, they themselves arranged to be picked up by practically every church that ran bus routes. Amazingly, they could tell a lot about the church they were about to attend by hopping the bus to get there.

For instance, if the driver was friendly, smiled and said hello, introducing Ambercrombie and Jason to a few of the kids on the bus, they knew the church was bound to be friendly. If the kids themselves seemed happy and engaged, they knew that the kids' ministry must be good. And if the volunteers assigned to the bus route greeted each kid and then interacted with them, playing games, telling jokes or singing songs on the way, then they knew that the teachers must also care about the kids.

On the other hand, they never revisited a church where the people working the bus weren't smiling or came across as being lackluster. Or if the kids themselves seemed bored or behaved like they had just been sent to detention.

Who needed the anguish?, Ambercrombie thought. And she kept up this proactive approach through high school, never actually settling on a particular denomination or place of worship. When she received her driver's license, she mainly used it to drive herself to a synagogue that was across town for weekly outreach services. The teachings were straight from the Torah, and the snacks provided, although Kosher, were top notch. (This was where she learned how good Hebrew National all-beef hot dogs were, convincing her parents to ditch their own brand preference.)

Freshman year of college, Ambercrombie got involved with an Intervarsity Fellowship-type group on campus that she found really thought-provoking. It didn't hurt that one of the leaders was your typical tall, dark and handsome sort, who had an eye for her. The feeling was mutual. Their first couple of dates were with other couples or groups which was a great way of finding out about someone without added pressure of one-on-one dating. On the way home from the third group outing, the luck of the draw turned out that the boy was driving Amercrombie back to her dorm alone. And as they pulled into the parking lot, he made an unsolicited pass that included physical touch that wasn't mutually appreciated. It wasn't until Ambercrombie actually slapped the boy, hard across the face, that he got the message.

In the relative scope of things, the would be make-out session that the boy intended didn't get much past proverbial first base, but it was enough to traumatize Ambercrombie, having come from a person she had completely trusted.

After college, she had dated a guy who professed to be a Christian, but after the fourth date, made it clear that he was of the "friends with benefits" type. She cut off the relationship without any incident, yet the gulf between professed belief and action bothered her, reinforcing a very strong reluctance towards actually joining a place of worship.

And by now, Ambercrombie had gotten into the habit of a round-robin approach to expressing her yearning for God. Hence the rating system she had developed on her chalkboard. Since she lived in a good-sized city, there was an endless supply of places to worship, so after a few of years using her tried-and-true system, she had barely begun to scratch the surface.

Back in Brenda's office, Lou gathered up his photos, minus the ones that Ambercrombie had selected.

"So, what's next?"

"We'll match up the photos with the cities in our guidebook, pretty much. And select one for the front cover. Then get back with you to see if we need any more shots. It should take about two weeks, tops."

"Then I can assume that you're going to use them?"

"Oh yeah. Lou, your work is excellent. It's just a matter of what order to put them in the guidebook. Brenda gave you our rate schedule, right?"

Lou nodded.

"Then, if you don't have any other questions, I think we're good for now."

"Actually, I do have one, if you don't mind."

"Sure."

"Would you like to have supper with me?"

Although the question was completely unexpected, it wasn't at all hard to answer. Lou was polite, engaging, and a very talented person. Who wouldn't mind that sort of company over a meal?

Two days later they met in a restaurant near her place of work.

After placing their orders, Lou started up the conversation. "So, there's a lot of pressure in the publishing business, I take it?"

"It's mostly the schedule of things. To make a profit you've always got to have five or six projects in the hopper simultaneously, and that's just hard cover. The move to self-publishing is great for new authors, but it's a killer to have to juggle that on top of traditional."

She continued: "What's it like being a professional photographer?"

Lou was surprised by Ambercrombie's question and responded by spitting out the water he had in his mouth.

"Sorry, but your last statement held quite an assumption."

"How so?"

"I'm not a professional photographer. That is, if you mean full time status. I love photography, but it's not what I'm doing to pay the bills right now."

"And that would be?"

"That would be driving a pick-up van for a day care center, along with working as a prep cook in the evenings."

Ambercrombie raised her eyebrows. "Quite a unique combination!"

"It is. The photography is a labor of love. When I get the chance, I take photos and try to sell them as a sideline. I've got a couple of buddies who are in the business so they give me leads. Right now I'm working on a series of shots of traditional church buildings."

As their waiter put their orders on the table, Ambercrombie remarked, "Not much of a fan of organized religion. I grew up with free-range parents and never really settled on one particular expression of faith."

"My Dad was an agnostic and Mom was a non-practicing Buddhist. But her parents were both evangelical Christians who grew up in the middle of the Jesus Movement in the 60s. They were a lot of fun and took me along with them when their church held special services. So because of their influence, when I moved out on my own I joined a church."

"Any regrets?"

"I wish we had better snacks after services."

"You're kidding! That's one of the things I use in my point system!"

"Point system?"

"I attend different churches to check them out and then when I get home, I rate them, according to a five point system that I sort of developed. My bedroom is filled with the results. So far, I've rated thirty-six."

"Wow, that must be some system."

Without missing a beat Ambercrombie continued: "It takes up almost an entire wall."

"Do you mind if I ask how long you've lived in the city?"

"About three years now. And I don't have geographic boundaries so I've gone to churches as far as 20 miles away. That's my limit because I have to attend small groups if they have them, and more than 20 miles on a weeknight would be a killer."

"Right."

"I've never told anyone that I do this sort of thing," she said, somewhat defensively. "You probably think I'm a little off."

"Actually, I don't. There can be quite a gulf between organized expression and individual belief. The fact that you've developed your own rating system shows you're serious about it."

"Absolutely!"

Lou paused a moment before continuing. "It also shows that it's highly likely that something or someone turned you off towards church in the past."

"Bingo."

"It's not much of a guess, Ambercrombie. You're going through a whole lot of extra work to explore something that a lot of church-goers take for granted."

The kindness in Lou's eyes led her to open up. "I've had a few bad experiences. Enough to keep me on the fence in regards to commitment. But what's weird is that I keep coming back."

"Nothing bad enough to keep you away?"

"I may not be a fan of organized religion, but I still love God."

"But you're still in a non-committal state of mind towards the whole issue?"

"Yeah, I guess so."

Lou was sitting straight up, continuing to pick at his meal but much more interested in pursuing the conversation he and Ambercrombie were having.

For her part, Ambercrombie hadn't really felt like discussing her views on religion with anyone. She had seen too much theological fisticuffs to think that there was much value to it. After all, what good was discussing something that seemed to be such a personal decision? Yet it was odd that Lou's questions didn't have the effect of shutting her down. In fact, he had inadvertently touched a wellspring that had been dammed up for too long.

"You're angry, then, about the religious scene?"

"More like a feeling of resentment."

"Interesting word choice."

"As in 'indignant displeasure at a perceived wrong,' according to Webster."

"Do you mind if I ask why?"

"At a couple of crucial points in my life, I was trusting Christian guys to show the love of God and instead they showed the love of my body. It wasn't really a huge deal, in regards to what they did physically, because I didn't allow them to get that far. But still, what they did was wrong, especially considering what they were supposed to believe."

"Where do you think resentment comes from?"

"Well, in my case, a deep-seated disappointment, of being let down, of someone not living up to an expected standard."

"I'm really sorry for your experience." Lou paused a bit before continuing. "How does it feel sitting on the fence when you're scoping out churches?"

Ambercrombie was about to say something like: "It feels fine." But what came out of her mouth was, "It feels frustrating. I'm part of a family for a while, worshipping and praying and flowing along with the service, but as soon as it ends, I want to be out of there. I bolt. I just can't stick around."

"It must be exhausting."

Her eyebrows shot up at Lou's use of such a word to describe her feelings "It is! There's a trade-off happening. I get to worship God in some way, and hear some good teaching, but I don't get the satisfaction of making connection with anyone in all of those churches that I visit."

"Because you were deeply offended, and you don't want to get hurt again."

"You know the old saying: 'fool me once, shame on you; fool me twice, shame on me.'"

Lou shook his head. "I had to look past my own parents' spiritual inertia to really become interested in God. But my grandparents helped me. They showed me that you can believe deeply in something and have a lot of fun at the same time."

"You have fun at your church, with your relationship with God?"

Lou's face lit up. "Oh yeah! One of the most amazing things I've learned is how to enjoy God together with a group. Whether it's singing, or listening to a teaching, or doing activities in the community. It's actually one of the most important lessons I've learned."

Now he had Ambercrombie genuinely intrigued. "But don't church members eventually do something that bothers you, or upsets you?"

"Sure they do, but people are people. Christians have to learn how to forgive each other, just like everyone else. God's used those hurtful times to teach me about grace."

Ambercrombie had heard the term before, but she wanted to be sure she understood Lou's meaning. "Define grace."

"It's unmerited favor. Freely given, totally undeserved. I mean, when you really examine it, that's the only way we get into relationship with God in the first place, isn't it?"

A smile slowly began to form on Ambercrombie's face as she let Lou's explanation sink in.

"Did I say something funny?"

"No, but I think you just helped me take a step towards getting off that fence."

Jennifer's Journal

Dustin was sitting next to Jennifer, a black-haired, blue-eyed woman in her late-20s, on the train to New York. They both were quiet. Other than asking if the empty seat next to hers was taken, Dustin hadn't said another word. He figured, don't hassle a female traveler. Besides, she was busy writing in her journal. After about an hour had passed, Jennifer excused herself to go to the diner car.

Although normally Dustin wasn't the snoopy type, he stole a glance at Jennifer's journal. Actually she had left it wide open on her seat, begging for someone to read: "I'm sitting next to this interesting looking guy, but he isn't much of a talker. He seems a bit stuck up to me."

Dustin had to laugh at that one. He had never had the opportunity to know, ahead of time, what any girl thought of him. Maybe it was the gentle rolling of the train that set his mind at ease, maybe it was the fact that train travel had always seemed adventurous. Whatever it was, He decided to get up and go to the dining car.

He found Jennifer sitting by herself, looking over a menu.

"Do you mind?" He asked, pointing to the empty seat, smiling.

"No, not at all." Jennifer smiled back cautiously.

"So, where are you headed?"

"New York City."

"In the movies they always ask, 'for business or pleasure?' Ultra suave conversation starter, isn't it?"

Jennifer laughed. Actually, it was more like a snort.

"Sorry, it's just that I've been up since five this morning, traveling from Dubuque. And it's sort of a little bit of both."

"Me too."

"A Cornhusker on the road to the Big Apple!"

"I hate to break the news to you, but you aren't a Cornhusker."

"Really now?"

"Not exactly. People from Iowa are Hawkeyes."

"I'll be gosh-darned! I graduated from Iowa, but I didn't really pay attention to the Big Ten thing. How about you?"

Jennifer was about to break out in a cold sweat. 'Gosh-darned!?' That was just great! She only reverted to Midwestern-speak when she was nervous.

Now it was Dustin's turn to laugh.

"Gosh-darned? What's next, gee-whiz?"

"Holy smokes comes before gee-whiz. Don't you remember anything your mother taught you?"

He reached out his hand to formally introduce himself. "I'm Dustin. From Michigan, but not as in the land of the Big Ten."

"Jennifer. And I come from the land of Lutherans who only laugh on weekends and paid holidays."

"So, what looks good?" he asked.

"Well, our waiter tells me that no one's died from the Your Mother's Meatloaf."

"But there's always a first time."

"Right. They don't tell you that in statistics class. Every single thing that ever occurred happened for the first time initially, and then, afterwards, it's all downhill."

"It doesn't have to be that way."

Jennifer arched her eyebrows.

"Look at Sisyphus. Do you think he complained about rolling that stupid ball up the hill all those times?"

"But that's a terrible example. It goes against your point."

"No it doesn't!"

"Actually, it does. Sisyphus was the most famously bored person ever."

Right at that moment, the waiter came and took Dustin and Jennifer's order. She went with Your Mother's Meatloaf with mashed potatoes and carrots. Dustin decided on the Salmon Surprise, which was a grilled salmon filet, encrusted with a light garlic potato breading, with a Mediterranean salad and rice.

Dustin picked up the conversation. "He gets a bad rap because no one understands what it's like to be patient anymore."

"Patient?"

"Yes. Patient."

"I thought Sisyphus was all about being condemned to drudgery."

Dustin shook his head. "He wasn't condemned. He was given an opportunity to learn patience."

"If you say so, Mr. English Major."

"Takes one to know one."

Jennifer smiled. Up until a half-hour ago, she was minding her own business, sitting in her seat, looking forward to what adventure awaited her in New York City. "What other majors do colleges offer these days?"

"Rocket science."

"Pardon?"

"How else can anyone check for authenticity whenever someone says, 'you know, it's not rocket science.'"

A huge smile crossed Jennifer's face. In a way, it was even better than her laugh. Because it was a little crooked and showed off her dimples at the same time. Very engaging, if you were the type who paid attention to that sort of thing. And growing up, Jennifer had been forced to pay attention to body language. It seemed like her mom and dad were always arguing, with the volume turned way, way up. In fact, her strongest childhood memories included those of hearing her mom and dad going at it downstairs. She could hear their accusations through the hot air register and it gave Jennifer her first doses of anxiety. But by the time she was five she had learned to overcompensate by developing her sense of humor. Anyone who spent time with her automatically received a free sample.

"So, when I arrive in Penn Station, I was thinking of checking out the restrooms to see if they have an opening for the next two nights. Nothing long term. But a girl's got to stay somewhere while she gets her feet planted."

"I take it you don't have family in Manhattan?"

"Actually, I have relatives in Brooklyn. Distant relatives." Jennifer put up both her hands. "O.K., they're my grandparents on my Dad's side. They came to America from the Ukraine. Which makes me second generation, once removed from the immigrant experience."

"How in the world did you wind up in Iowa?"

Immediately Dustin experienced a surge of regret. What a loaded question. How does anyone wind up anywhere? Sometimes it was actually the result of forethought and careful planning. But it could also be the end product of a series of accidents, a marriage, a job, or a deep desire to put some distance between you and someone else. In Dustin's experience, it was rarely well thought out. Case in point; Dustin was on a train headed to New York because he was frustrated with his writing. He had submitted tons of short stories, and had acquired an impressive collection of rejection slips. Meanwhile, he had been working for the local daily newspaper to pay the bills, but it had recently been bought out by one of those media conglomerates which halved the staff overnight. Being the author of a twice weekly column along with an assigned human interest beat hadn't saved him from the axe. So, he thought: I'm 33 years old. It's now or never. I'm energetic enough to start from scratch in a new city. Better strike while the iron is hot.

Besides, his severance package included the equivalent of a half a year's salary. So, *tempis fugit* and all that. The point was that Dustin picked up his final check the morning he was let go, went to the bank, told his roommate he was leaving, packed his bags, and headed to the train station. That was all the thought he had put into it.

"Well, my grandparents were a tad eccentric," answered Jennifer. "They refused to learn English and didn't venture out of the neighborhood at all. Manhattan might as well have been Micronesia. Grandpa and Grandma tried very hard to instill a fear of the unknown in my dad, but it had the very opposite effect on him. He was an only child and probably would have been adventurous anyway. But having two parents who were so morosely tied to the old country only fueled his desire to get as far away as possible. So, when he was sixteen, he lied to the recruiter, doctored up his birth certificate and joined the Navy."

"Vietnam?

"The tail end of it. Fortunately, Dad got there a week after Saigon fell. So he was part of a small fleet that surreptitiously patrolled the Pacific for two years. He was very lucky. And after his tour of duty was up, he re-enlisted, got the GI Bill, and applied to Iowa State. He met my mom there and got a degree in medicine."

"Your Dad's a doctor, as in MD?"

"Yeah, as in MD. And my Mom teaches at the Iowa Writers' Workshop."

"Yikes!"

"Tell me about it. She's read more good-but-not-brilliant writing than a human should have to in ten lifetimes. But she's able to encourage and offer insight. She's an amazing woman in the classroom. But by the time I was born, my parents realized they had both married out of a romanticized version of what marriage should be. And since no relationship is perfect, it only accentuated their differences. Dad was very ethnic. Mom was a real all-American WASP. So once I was born they began to fight constantly. Which only goes to prove that even successful professionals can be really messed up. How about your parents?"

Dustin coughed. It was a reflex he had developed to give

himself time to decide if he wanted to answer whenever anyone asked him about his family. He quickly decided Jennifer was genuinely interested.

"It's a boring story really. Boy and girl from the same small town grow up as next door neighbors. But their families don't particularly get along. So to continue seeing each other they decide to go to Michigan State. He becomes a CPA. She becomes a lawyer. They stay in East Lansing stay in love and have a family and make tons of money. Meanwhile one of their sons grows up thinking he's adopted because he can't get enough of language arts. He eventually becomes a journalist."

Jennifer shook her head in mock sadness. "Isn't that the way it goes? They're always growing up to be journalists aren't they?"

"Right."

"Aren't parental expectations the best!"

"What's the statute of limitations on blaming your parents for everything that goes wrong in life?"

She thought a minute before answering. "In the 70's it used to be twenty-one, but nowadays it's been pushed forward to thirty-seven."

"Wow! That's a relief!"

"Yeah. I've got a few years to go yet. I better start learning how to take the fall for my own mistakes, eh?"

(It can be very hard to detach yourself from the emotional legacy of a family. Sometimes it means a shunning that outdoes the Amish. In the end, compromises are struck.)

When their meal was served, they ate for a few minutes in silence. Neither of them had eaten any real food since early morning. But as soon as their dinner began to settle, they picked up the conversation, with Jennifer starting up.

"I think a big part of the growing up process is pretty simple. Nobody goes through their 20s scot-free. You're either disentangling yourself from all the academic mumbo-jumbo they throw at you in college, or else you're hanging out with your friends, working at something that barely affords you enough to split the rent with a person or two, or else you've lucked out and married straight out of college, know exactly what you want to do and begin a family. In which case you are working too hard and are so involved with your family that thinking about life becomes a luxury."

"Ironic, isn't it? That the only people who aren't over analyzing their life are the ones who are too busy living it."

"So which are you?"

Dustin knew he wasn't about to touch that one with a ten foot pole. He considered himself lucky that he had gotten out of college relatively scar free. He wasn't one to needlessly analyze. Maybe it was because he knew he was very, very fortunate to have had two parents who genuinely loved each other. He had seen, firsthand, what a solid marriage looked like, and it was both a curse and a blessing. A blessing because he had an extraordinary understanding of its importance and had benefited greatly from a house where there was such strong love among the family members. And it was a curse because Dustin knew what marriage could be, and he was unwilling to settle for anything less.

"Well, first I have to say that I'm extremely lucky."

"How's that?" Jennifer pushed herself back from the table and sat up straight. She was looking right at Dustin.

"Because I grew up in a family where love was expressed every day. I sort of took it for granted, but now I can see how much it strengthened me."

"How did it strengthen you?"

"For openers, I tend to think positively about things. I try to look on the bright side and I don't let myself get distracted about things I can't control or change. Which, turns out to be, most everything."

Jennifer laughed. "Wow. So, you hung out in Mister Rogers' Neighborhood?"

"Something like that. I mean, we had our moments, but

they weren't things we fought about. They were just differences. Maybe that's one of the more important lessons I learned from my family. Tolerance for others and their point of view."

"But isn't tolerance just another name for apathy? For a milky blending of everyone else's way of life?"

Dustin had no familial reference for heated, vocal arguments. Because of his own grandparents' lack of grace, his parents had maintained a respectful distance from them. When grandchildren came, visitation rights were hinged on being polite. Even if it was superficial, at first, eventually, genuine affection towards the grandchildren spilled over to the parents.

"I'm not sure about that," he said. "I think it boils down to choosing your fights."

At last, thought Jennifer, we're reaching some common ground! "Exactly! So you're offering a proverb that speaks to the importance of venting! My own family is a classic example of not being able to differentiate between what's worth fighting for and what's not. But at least it points to the fact that fighting is inevitable. Summoning the words of the last President-who-was-assassinated Kennedy, 'I don't shrink from this responsibility, I welcome it!'"

"So you're saying that you like to fight?"

"I'm saying that we're human, and that's something that humans do, and we shouldn't be afraid of it."

Their waiter came and cleared the table, offering another natural lull in the conversation.

"What's the purpose then of fighting?" Dustin asked.

"Clearing the air! Getting whatever you're fighting about out in the open! Having a chance of emotional healing."

"Really? I mean, about the emotional healing part? How often have you overheard people saying nasty things to each other and then regretting it?"

"The process of reconciliation is part of the beauty of it. That negative emotion, if given a chance to express itself, can result in healing. I see it all the time."

"You do?"

"Yeah. I'm a grief counselor."

"And you encourage your clients to get angry?"

"I encourage them to admit their anger as the first step towards letting go of it. I never said I advocated fighting as a lifestyle."

"Point taken." This was getting interesting, thought Dustin. Who would have thought that sitting next to a stranger on a train would have wound up like this? Ordinarily he would have been perfectly content to spend the travel time to himself; more often than not a good book had been his best friend. But in a flash, he realized what a mistake that would have been.

"So, you're a professional counselor?"

"Yes."

"Well, I don't know if this is kismet, or what, but usually, I don't invite myself to dinner with someone that I don't know."

"I could tell that from the way you asked me if you could sit next to me when you came on the train."

"That's why you thought I was stuck up?"

Jennifer laughed. "Do you always read other people's personal journals?"

"Only when the writer keeps them wide open, facing me when they leave their seat."

She laughed again. "Yeah, well, I thought you were interesting, or else I wouldn't have accepted your invitation."

"So, what's next?"

"How about we have ourselves dessert?" Jennifer said laughing.

The Librarian

Ella was working her rotation on the circulation desk. She was the head librarian in a small town facility that had about 10,000 volumes, plus local newspapers and a few national magazines on the racks. It was the sort of library that was bordered by the town square, which was actually quite beautiful.

She had been wondering lately if what she did made a difference. Who really cared that deeply about renewing their library card, or that the stacks were always kept current? She had a "get them back in the stacks within 24 hours" goal and in her 14 years on the job, she had always kept it. Each morning she diligently checked "research request" emails to be sure that they were promptly answered, imagining that each sender had already googled themselves silly while trying to obtain answers and had turned to her as a last resort.

The Youth Corner was always kept clean and up-to-date. How else to engage that generation with the importance of reading and learning? To this end, Ella hosted a monthly get-together to discuss the selected teen novel. It was never on the current bestseller list. Usually it was a book considered a classic or something equally obscure that most teens would never, on their own, seek out. She actually found herself getting excited at the reality of helping to broaden their experience with literature.

Ella was equally engaged with the senior population of Elk

Grove, paying particular attention to the six computer terminals that were available for patrons to use. She had implemented a policy for them of unlimited time, as long as there wasn't a queue for use. In turn, many of that generation had thanked her profusely for helping them set up email accounts and familiarize themselves with the various software programs that she taught in the afternoon sessions.

The truth was that Ella had sort of stumbled upon the librarian job in the first place. Her degree was in archeology with a minor in English literature, but after graduation, the job market wasn't exactly overflowing with offers. That, combined with the timing of Doris' (the former head librarian) retirement, led to her current position. There were no regrets on her part. From a very young age she had always felt at home in the town library. She had seen it as a refuge from her home environment. The quietness of the place had been a haven to her. The neat, orderly stacks of books, the wonderful solitude was actually invigorating to her.

For a small town Elk Grove had been extremely supportive of the librarian position, even to the extent of paying for the additional courses she had taken in library science to supplement all that she had learned from the previous director, who had willingly offered to stay on part-time, for three months, in order to guide Ella into the position.

"There's no place like this," Doris had told her. "This is your kingdom and you can make it as inviting and peaceful as possible." In her three decades of leading the library, Doris had seen hundreds upon hundreds of children come through the front door's with an eagerness in their eyes that was absolutely delicious. Each day as she looked beyond the circulation desk, she vowed to do all she could to keep that excitement alive. As far as Doris was concerned, this was the most important thing she had endeavored to pass along to Ella.

So here Ella was, 37 years of age, applying furniture polish to the desks by the reference section early on a Thursday morning before she opened up the doors for business. (This was, after all, a small town library, one in which the head librarian was also part custodian, special events coordinator, and counselor.)

Later that same morning, she had a scheduled meeting with Duncan Fraizer, who owned the mill. For 20 years Duncan had overseen the biggest employer in town. He was an exceedingly generous person, having learned that trait from both his parents. They knew the importance of owning the town's biggest business and never took its success for granted.

After opening up the doors and greeting her assistant librarian and checkout specialist, Ella walked the two short blocks down Water Street to the mill and knocked on Duncan's door. She had arranged the meeting to ask if Duncan would be interested in supporting a capital campaign that included adding a community room to the library, as well as various other upgrades.

"Come on in!" he said. He was a self-assured yet very down-to-earth sort of person. The kind who immediately put people at ease. This had helped him in wooing his wife, Amy, 55 years ago; a union which had produced one son, Thom.

"Good morning, Duncan."

"So, how goes it?"

"Fine! And you?"

"Couldn't be better. What's on your mind?" He motioned for Ella to have a seat.

Ella gave a brief overview of the capital campaign she had in mind. Duncan was naturally her first 'ask.' His reputation in the community was solid, and if he lent his support, others in town would quickly follow his example.

"So," asked Ella. "What do you think? Can the Library count on your support?"

Duncan paused a moment, twiddling his pencil in-between his fingers. Which was something he always did when mulling over a decision.

"Well, you know Dad and Mom always supported the

Library. I have very fond memories of going there in grade school to pick up books, and you know I still use it. It's actually my go-to place to relax so I can think things through."

Actually Duncan's senior staff knew that whenever there was an important business decision to be made, they could find him at the Library. There was a jar of money that sat on his secretary's desk that held the bets among staff as to where to find Duncan during the week. The money was never collected, but used towards the office Christmas party.

He scratched his head before continuing: "So, I'd have to say that investing in the Library's capital campaign is a small way to pay you back. You've got my support. In fact, put us down for sixty-five percent of the total cost."

What a relief! Ella stood up, smiled, and shook Duncan's hand. "Thank you! I knew I could count on you, but I wasn't expecting such an outstanding commitment." She turned towards the door, but then, on impulse, looked back towards him. "Where would this town be without you!"

Duncan only smiled, and turned red with embarrassment. He wasn't one to tout his position and he certainly wasn't the type to go fishing for accolades. "Ella, this company has done really, really well over the years. I have to believe that it's because my parents taught me to put others first. And that includes this town. To them Elk Grove was the people who live in it, and they absolutely loved this place."

He had been all over the world engaging friends who became customers. In doing so, he had the opportunity to touch down in some amazing cities. But for all the culture and beauty he had seen beyond Elk Grove's borders, it was Elk Grove that still captured his heart. He had been given the opportunity to move his family and the family business on numerous occasions, but each time he quickly realized it was a "no brainer" to stay put.

As Ella walked back to the Library, she thought that her next ask would be Thom. He had worked for his dad for a few years out of college, and then, with his dad's support, struck out on his own to form a material handling equipment business that served not only his dad, but just about every production facility within a 50 mile radius.

Thom was just as business oriented as his father, but like many children of prominent people, struggled with his own self-worth. As a young boy, he had been on the shy side and didn't have much of a social life. He came across as being rather serious, but the fact was, under the right circumstances, he could be anything but.

The next day, Ella drove over to Thom's company, which was a couple of miles outside of town. In her phone call to him, she had said very little about the reason for the visit, thinking it best to feel him out first. She had been a classmate of Thom's from kindergarten through high school, but they had seldom seen each other outside of the classroom. Ella's family was too distracted by their own internal strife to recognize the need for their daughter's social life, and Duncan and Amy's circle of friends, although wide, didn't include Ella's parents.

It only took Thom a moment to answer the knock on his office door.

"Hey, nice to see you!" Truth be told, he had been an admirer of hers from afar during their senior year. But you know how that sort of thing usually goes if one of the potential partners is shy and prone to steering clear of the opposite sex.

"Good to see you too, Thom!"

"What's up?"

"Well, I should ask if you'd had a chance to chat with your dad recently."

"Not really. Dad's been busy and things have been going strong on this end too."

"I talked with him yesterday about the Library."

"You did?"

"I gave him an overview about our capital campaign. It includes a new community room and some necessary upgrades."

Thom raised his eyebrows and smiled. "Go on."

"And after I gave him some of the details, he agreed to be our first supporter."

"Sounds like Dad. You know he really loves our Library."

"He does. So I thought a natural second ask would be you." She then began to tell him some of the details of the campaign.

One of Thom's earliest library memories was cradling up with a picture book in the children's nook, which still had a large stained glass window of Mother Goose. In high school he had found Woody Allen's "Without Feathers," in the stacks and remembered laughing out loud while reading it. He was also thinking how beautifully sincere Ella looked. Even when they had been in grade school, it struck him how she had this unusual determination about her. But back then, he only marked it down to temperament, and not intelligence. As they grew into adults, he could plainly see her genuine love of others was at the root of any project she chose to get involved with.

"So, what do you say Thom?"

From out of nowhere she visualized what Thom would be like as a father. She imagined him to be just as thoughtful and kind at home as he was everywhere else. He would teach his children patience and the importance of putting others first by the way he treated his family. The feeling that this image brought up was so strong that Ella began to tear up.

"Are you ok?"

"Yes," she began to apologize, quickly trying to cover for herself. "Seasonal allergies, that's all."

He handed her a box of tissues. "You're very good."

"At what?" she asked, pulling out one of the tissues. Ella had her own insecurities. She had inherited a deep sense of unworthiness, picking it up almost by emotional osmosis, from being around parents who just didn't know how to support each other. She had gone out to see a film once where a high school teacher had told one of his students: "We accept the love we think we deserve." That line had been a revelation to Ella. As soon as the words were spoken she felt as if someone had hit her in the chest with the proverbial ton of bricks. She had gasped out loud and was glad that no one was sitting close enough to witness the waterfall of tears that cascaded down her checks afterwards.

"You gave a pretty good presentation, Ella. There really isn't any reason why I wouldn't join my Dad in supporting the Library. I don't know what he pledged, but put me down for twenty-five percent."

Thom then wondered why he had never asked Ella on a date. How could someone like another person, in the romantic sense, and not follow up on it? How could a person sit still for an entire senior year, day in and day out, and watch graduation getting closer by the second and not speak up? It had been a surreal experience, to say the least. Like watching yourself performing in a bad play – you wanted to scream: "Get out! Just get out of there! Do something!" But you were powerless to pull yourself away. Why was it only in this particular aspect of his life, that Thom felt so defeated? He saw the love his parents had for each other. He had seen tons of friends date and develop the social skills necessary to engage potential life partners, but none of it had rubbed off on him. In college he was the studious type, and since that was what came naturally to him, he used it as a convenient excuse to not date. His grades were among the top in each class he took, but on weekends, when his friends went out he could be found in the dorm lounge doing extra work.

How does something that is so simple for most of the human race become impossible? This is absolutely ridiculous, thought Thom. I turned out to be so socially inept. I never took the chance when I was younger and now I'm paying the price for it. Doing good and liking people doesn't automatically result in women beating a path to your doorway.

In fact, there had been a few girls who had made it plain that they were interested in him, but Thom's response had been one of disbelief. And he had yet to figure out exactly why, other than having a tremendous insecurity when it came to women.

"Thanks Thom," Ella said, smiling. "You and your dad

are making this really easy. Which is good, because I'm not a fundraiser!" She laughed.

She wanted to tell him that she remembered the day of their graduation, and how he had awkwardly told her that he would be attending a college out of state, turning beet red in the process. Normally he was fine with relaying information like that on a friend-to-friend basis, but when it came to going beyond that, she could tell it was difficult for him. She had wanted to ease his mind, to do or say something that would calm him down. But she had problems of her own. So instead of saying: "Hey Thom, we should stay in touch with each other," what came out of her mouth was: "That's really great! I'm sure you'll have a lot of wonderful experiences!" She had also told him that she would be going to the state college only 35 miles away because she had gotten a full scholarship and that was the only way she could afford to go.

Despite feeling comfortable with him, she had never taken the first step towards an intimate conversation. The kind where she could have shared what was happening at home. She hadn't told any of her girlfriends, let alone a boy. And the holding back had kept her from experiencing deep conversation that only comes with the letting go of secrets.

She began to leave Thom's office, turning away from him.

All of sudden something moved inside him. It wasn't like an earthquake. It was more like a small crack. Enough of a crack that he recognized the moment as an opportunity. He realized that he was about to embark on uncharted territory, but the crack had changed his normal response. Instead of balking, instead of holding back, instead of remaining helplessly inert at the path that led from friendship to something deeper, he began to speak up. For the first time in his life, he allowed his heart to beat fast in Ella's presence without choosing to squelch it.

"Ella?"

She turned towards him. She had no idea why her usual response of pushing aside any invitation to go deeper wasn't working. It wasn't as if she and Thom hadn't had tons of opportunities just like this before. But there had been an unspoken rule between them. They respected each other's awkwardness and that meant never talking about it. This had been the foundation upon which they had become friends.

"By any chance, are you free for lunch sometime?" (Was he going too fast? Was he going to blow her out of the water with such a brazen invitation? In their years of knowing each other, of bumping into each other at meetings, or on the street, he had never, ever asked such a question. He was fidgeting now, but remained determined to press on.)

Ella turned and smiled again. For her part, she also realized that her heart was kicking into overtime. She thought: Man, it feels like I just went for a five mile run. Talk about boldly going where no one has gone before! If I say yes, he might think I'm being completely forward. He might be disappointed enough to cancel altogether. I've read where this sort of thing gets easier with age, but whoever made that observation obviously doesn't know our history!

"Thom, I really don't want to disappoint." Now she'd gone and done it! Despite her best efforts, Thom's question had been so out-of-the-blue that a second wave, this time of social terror, came over her. She could feel the ground shaking beneath her and she reached out to lean against the doorframe to keep from falling.

"Are you alright?"

She blurted out, "This is weird, isn't it?"

"Having lunch together?"

"No, I mean, we're about to break the code here; you realize that, don't you?"

"So?"

"Thom, this is me. And this is you. And we've never gotten this far with each other before in all these years."

"So?"

"Are you being contrary on purpose?"

Thom took a deep breath. Ella had just given him a perfect opportunity to bail out with a retraction. But this time, he wasn't the slightest bit interested in chickening out. Instead he laughed.

"I'm not being contrary; I'm asking, despite the weirdness, if you'd like to take a chance and see what would happen if we had lunch. You know, like normal people."

"But we've never been normal that way."

"Who says we can't approach it like us?"

Her heart was slowing down a bit, which was a good sign. At least she could continue the conversation and not reply with some lamebrain excuse to get out of it.

"Like us?"

Thom continued "Yeah. Who says we have to exude mass amounts of self-confidence before we can take a first step? We can admit it's scary and not get freaked out about it, can't we? Isn't that one of the advantages of being adults and not high schoolers?"

Ella smiled back. "Insecurity can actually be sexy, can't it?" She inadvertently took a step backwards and almost tripped. "So is falling over your own feet, I've heard."

He had to admit that he had always loved her smile. Especially given in friendship, it was warm and inviting and shy all at once. "Is that a yes, then?"

She took her hand off the doorframe and straightened herself up. "Well, usually, by now I would have come up with something and politely turned down the invite. You know, something like, 'I'm booked solid for the next two months. I'll have to get back to you.'"

"Or 'I have allergies to human food so I don't eat in restaurants.'"

"'There's a full moon coming up, so I really shouldn't.'"

"'I can't eat out during the high holy days.'"

"I didn't know you were Jewish."

"I'm not."

"How about 'I'm a vegan and there's no place I can eat out within thirty miles of here.'"

"You're a vegan?"

"No."

They both laughed.

"So I guess this means we're having lunch at some point."

Slowly she shook her head 'no.'

"Now what?"

"Not at some point, Thom. Today!"

Reanette

The first memory that Reanette had was of crawling past her mom, who was ironing clothes at the end of the house that had steps leading to the back door. Reanette was in diapers and was determined to do an end-run past her mom, who hadn't noticed her youngest daughter was scooting around. There wasn't any way that a safety gate could be affixed to the entire section of railing above the six foot drop off. So, in her enthusiasm, Reanette wound up crawling onto thin air and falling, head first, onto the cement floor below. She remembered lifting her head up to see her mom running down the steps, and the look of terror on her face, and thinking: Wow, something must have gotten Mom really upset. Then she lost consciousness.

Throughout her life, Reanette would occasionally jolt back to that drop. When she was first outfitted for glasses in junior high school, the ophthalmologist who examined her noted that she had a particularly unusual astigmatism. It meant that she wore glasses with two distinct lenses. The right lens had practically no strength to it at all, but the left lens was a different story, looking, from a distance, like a magnifying glass.

"You're going to have an adjustment wearing your glasses," the doctor had said after the initial examination.

"Why?" she casually asked.

"There's quite a difference between your eyes' ability to focus. Do you remember anything that could have caused that?"

"Well, when I was in diapers, I crawled off the edge of the floor and fell onto concrete."

It was then that Reanette figured she must have fallen on the left side of her head. She also figured out that she was ambidextrous – at least enough to bat left-handed when playing baseball, and if she had taken up golfing, she would have used left-handed clubs. Most everything else she did with her right hand.

The next memory that stuck out in Reanette's mind was swinging on the backyard swing set. It actually was just one swing that faced the next-door neighbor's yard. She was nearly three and had recently learned how to propel herself back and forth for the first time. The movement was exhilarating, feeling the motion deep down in the pit of her stomach. Equally fun was looking up at the sky and watching the clouds drift by as she drew up closer, seemingly on her way to leaving the earth. These sensations were so vivid that Reanette would continue to swing into adulthood, with the same fervency.

In fact, using swing sets was one of Reanette's favorite activities. But it didn't transfer over to roller-coasters or other carnival rides. Each summer during the Fourth of July a carnival came to town. The crowds, combined with the barkers running the games along the narrow aisles, caused her to be claustrophobic.

Another not so favorite memory was of her parents' arguing.

"You're absolutely the most ignorant person on the face of the earth!" her father would yell to start things off. "You're repulsive."

At first Reanette found it confusing, being so young. She had no idea, at the time, what exactly her dad was accusing her mom of, but she felt, if he said it, then it must be true.

When Reanette was about to begin first grade, her parents had decided to have a neighborhood party, inviting all the other kids who were Reanette's age. Normally, a child would remember the party itself and the games played, or fun had with the other kids, but that wasn't highlighted in her memory of it. Her sense of that day began with an image of being cradled underneath the dining room table, sensing that her parents were about to unload at any moment. Thankfully, Dixon, a friend the same age as Reanette, who lived a few houses down the street, came to her rescue by crawling next to her.

"Hey what are you doing down here?" he asked.

"Avoiding people," she had told him.

"Isn't the point of having a party to be with them?"

"I wouldn't actually know about that."

"Why not?"

"This is the first party I've ever been to in my life."

"Well how's it going so far from down here?" he asked, giving her a smile.

"Not so great."

Dixon smiled even broader as he gave his hand to Reanette. "Well then, what do you say we blow this popcorn stand?"

Reanette hadn't heard the expression before, and the way that Dixon said it caused her to laugh out loud.

"Come on," he said, clarifying. "Let's go outside."

They walked through the kitchen, out the back door, and up the alley to a park that stood on a hill overlooking the town. Dixon nodded towards a bench and tried to change the subject.

"So, are you excited about starting first grade?"

Reanette shook her head and threw out her hands, palms upturned. (It would be a few years before she learned the word 'exasperation,' but in the meantime, the outward sign worked.)

"What's the point?"

"What do you mean?"

"I've been having this dream over and over again where I don't have to leave my house to go to school. And I'm learning really cool things too." (This was happening in the days before home school was allowed in her home state.)

"But what about the new kids that we'll meet there? It'll be like kindergarten, only better."

"I hated kindergarten. There were too many rules and having to take a nap after lunch was boring."

"In first grade we get to learn about lots of different subjects."

"Such as?"

"Like reading and writing and spelling and social studies. Trust me, you're going to love it."

"Just as much as I like okra, huh?"

"Right!"

"Dixon, I can't stand okra. I don't like the smell of it; I don't even like the idea of it. When my family goes to a restaurant and there's okra on the menu, I want to barf."

Actually, Reanette's family never went out to eat. They didn't go much of anywhere as a family until her mom and dad split up, but that hadn't happened yet. She was fairly outgoing with her own siblings, but was cautious while getting to know others. Although she knew that the tense atmosphere in her own home was unusual, she never told anyone about it, because she thought sharing family information in public was brash.

Dixon, on the other hand, was a real social butterfly. He was an only child, which made him a bit on the precocious side, spending the majority of his time at home in the company of adults. In the neighborhood he tended to roam to any house that had kids near his age. He was affable to a fault, but yet he wasn't one to let others push him into doing something he didn't want to do.

"OK, I get it, but you don't have to be sarcastic about it, do you?"

"What's sarcastic?"

"It's behaving the way you are now. Being so angry and frustrated that all you can do is make fun of it."

"What else is there to do? I'm not an adult, I can't fix it."

At the time, Reanette hadn't yet confided her family secret to Dixon. So he had no idea of her family's situation. All he knew was that something was making Reanette tense. And he wished with all his six-year-old heart that he could help.

When Reanette was in fourth grade, one beautiful July day she could tell that her parents were about to explode again. By this time, she had grown weary of the family drama, so she simply told her older brother that she was going down the street for a visit. When Dixon answered the door, he immediately noticed that she had been crying and took her to the backyard.

"What's going on?"

"Oh, the usual," when Reanette said this she looked away from Dixon because she started to cry again.

He gently turned Reanette's face towards his until their eyes met. "Can you tell me what it is?" He pulled out a handkerchief and handed it to her. As far as Reanette knew, Dixon was the only boy who carried one.

That very act of kindness caused her to unload a childhood's worth of sadness. "My family isn't normal."

"Whose is?"

"I mean, it's awful the way that my parents don't get along."

"That sucks, doesn't it?"

For some reason Dixon's comment struck Reanette as funny. So she went from sobbing to letting out peals of laughter. At first Dixon thought that his friend was going crazy, but then he realized the value of releasing pent-up frustration by laughing.

"Yeah, it does," she said, after she had collected herself. "Thanks for the hankie."

"No problem. I guess I knew something was up, but I had no idea about your mom and dad."

"I never heard you use that word, 'suck,' before. Are you taking slang lessons at the Y?"

"My family doesn't have a membership there."

"I'm being sarcastic."

"So, what's the answer? How can you make the situation better?"

"Click my heels three times and say 'there's no place like home?'"

Dixon stared at her until Reanette punched him in the arm.

"I'm being sarcastic again, ok?"

This was how Reanette decided to deal with the situation until her parents started divorce proceedings. By that time, she had learned the meaning of the word 'resentment' fairly well. In fact, by the time Reanette was a senior in high school, she was very good at feeling indignant towards her parents. Even though the divorce had definitely improved her home life, she was still experiencing the emotional aftershocks of childhood trauma.

As fate would have it, Reanette and Dixon drifted apart during high school. It was a combination of different class schedules, different interests, and both having to work to save up money for college. By this time, Reanette and her family had moved across town, so she no longer had an opportunity to see Dixon simply by walking down the street to his house.

So it was the first week of their freshman year of college. Reanette was sitting outside of the Michigan State student union, minding her own business, soaking in the sun, waiting for friends to join her for lunch. The sun's warmth was inviting and was just about to coax her to sleep, when she heard someone calling her name. She opened her eyes and could hardly believe who was standing there.

"Dixon?" He had changed in the four years since they had almost daily contact with each other, but not enough to leave him unrecognizable.

He shrugged and opened up his arms in a "got me" stance. "How are you, Reanette?"

"I'm good, I mean, how are you? I can't believe it's you."

"I'm fine. So, you're attending school here too?"

Reanette nodded and motioned for him to sit down.

"Well, let me take a good look. You have really grown up nicely."

Dixon felt himself blushing. "So have you. This is a little awkward, isn't it?"

"Yeah. I don't know what happened between us. When my family moved across town, I had no way to see you and I really didn't want to go back to the old neighborhood, you know."

"I completely understand. You were busy, life happens."

"No, Dixon. I was devastated. My family was torn apart. I sort of got into a bad place after that."

"I really missed you. I wanted to reach out, but I had no idea where you went and you were part of another crowd, and I couldn't seem to catch your attention. It was weird how our paths never seemed to cross. A few times I'd see you waiting for the bus after school, but after a while, it was plain that you'd moved on."

"I am so sorry."

"Friendships don't usually last forever. That's the way it is."

"Now you're the one who's being sarcastic."

Wouldn't you have loved it if the two of them had been able to sort out their mutual feelings of resentment, right then and there? But this isn't a love story, at least not that kind of one. Their serendipitous meeting as college freshmen wasn't enough to salve over four lost years - years in which Reanette's childhood feelings for Dixon had remained intact, but forgotten. Meanwhile, to say that Dixon's young heart had been demolished by Reanette's sudden absence would be an understatement. Something from Shakespeare comes to mind:

> "Oh how her eyes and tears did lend and borrow!
> Her eyes seen in the tears, tears in her eye;
> Both crystals where they view'd each other's sorrow,
> Sorrow that friendly sighs sought still to dry;
> But like a stormy day, now wind, now rain,
> Sighs dry her cheeks, tears make them wet again."

Michigan State has a huge campus, big enough to keep long lost friends apart if they don't share a common curriculum or if they lived off campus to save money. Dixon was a biology major and had been accepted into MSU's School of Veterinary Medicine. Reanette was double-majoring in elementary education and psychology. It was their senior year, a few days before Christmas break. The library was full of students pulling all nighters. Dixon had been holed up for six straight hours and he needed to get out and get some fresh air. He packed his books into his backpack and headed out the door to his favorite Mexican place on Grand River.

The restaurant was packed. Ordinarily he would have turned around and headed out the door, but he craved rice and beans with a side of guacamole. So, he took a deep breath, spied a vacant seat by a table for two and went for it. He could tell, as he approached the table from the backside, that the other seat was occupied by a blonde haired woman.

"Excuse me," he asked, "but is that seat taken?"

The woman answered without turning. "No, feel free."

As Dixon moved to take his seat, he found he was sitting across the table from Reanette.

"I am so sorry," he began. "I didn't know it was you. I can try to find another seat."

"Don't be silly. You're probably just about to collapse from over-studying for finals, right?"

"Truer words were never spoken."

"Then please, sit down."

After the waiter came to take his order, Dixon picked up the conversation.

"This really is odd isn't it? I've been wondering how you're doing actually."

"As in curiosity killed the cat?"

"Something like that, yes."

"Well, I've got a double major in elementary education and psychology."

"Wow, that's got to keep you busy!"

"It does, but I want to be able to influence the lives of the kids that I'm teaching. I don't want them winding up like me."

"What do you mean?"

"I've done a lot of thinking since high school, about my family and those early years. It was such an awful time, and I had no one to talk to about it, except you. And I didn't even tell you what was going on until my parents were practically divorced."

Dixon sensed that Reanette needed to get something off her chest, so he nodded but kept quiet.

"You have no idea how sorry I am that our friendship turned out the way that it did. My leaving so suddenly wasn't my idea. You have to know that, Dixon. Your friendship meant the world to me and you were one of the most important people in my life."

"I understand."

"I guess that's where the double major comes in. I want to have the tools to help kids whose home lives are messed up. I want to be able to reach out to them before it's too late."

"That's really admirable."

She looked at him and took a deep breath. Four years lost in high school. College almost lost altogether, as far as their friendship was concerned. She figured it was now or never. She wasn't going to play it safe by holding back.

"I've missed you Dixon."

During his sophomore year at MSU, Dixon had started to attend a Christian fellowship, where he had learned that mercy trumps resentment. At least, in his case, it had released Dixon from an emotional prison where he had kept Reanette as hostage. For her part, Reanette had come to appreciate the many positive parts of her parents that showed up in her own DNA.

He continued the conversation: "I need to apologize for the way that I acted our freshman year; that conversation in front of the Student Union never should have turned out that way. I was still pretty hurt from what happened when you moved away. But you didn't deserve my attitude."

She smiled and reached out across the table, gently punching Dixon on the arm. "We both messed up. But we're here now."

"And we've both learned what lies on the opposite end of resentment."

Reanette's smile was even broader now, her face positively radiant. "Forgiveness."

Colorado in the Morning

Suny was sitting on the front porch looking out at the bed of columbines in the front yard.

One of the first things she had done when she bought the house was to tear out a good portion of the front lawn and plant perennials. Among them, columbines seemed to be her favorite. They had long, graceful stems which led to a brilliant purple blossom. For some reason she considered the leaves to be hopeful. Maybe because they reminded her so much of super-sized clover.

At any rate, here she was, 15 years after moving to a place outside Boulder, wondering how she got there. At the time, anything had seemed better than Grand Junction, Michigan. Suny had grown up there, went through the town's school system, gone on to college, where she majored in general studies while taking as many pottery classes as she could. In the end, the only thing that had made much sense to her was the potter's wheel, and the feel of the clay's smoothness yielding to the slightest pressure from her hands.

In time she had learned to let her fingertips remain supple while building up the strength in her palms. Actually it wasn't as much a technique that she had picked up from anyone as much as it was a sort of natural, common-sense revelation. Why wouldn't you let you hands guide you, they're doing all the work anyway.

So here Suny sat, amazed with how life works itself out. She was equally amazed at the fawn that was curiously sniffing her lavender a few feet away from the edge of the front yard flower bed. I wish I could run a glaze that had such beautiful spots in it, she was thinking. The deer looked up, straight at her, and for a split second seemed to be smiling. Until Buddy, one of her cats, long-haired, with black and white splotches, cutely short, spooked it.

"Buddy! Come back here!"

The cat immediately stopped running towards the fawn, turned and ran back, its large, fluffy tail waving lazily in the air.

Suny thought: Isn't it curious how cats can change their moods so quickly? They can move from purring to nipping at you in a second. As if to prove her point, Buddy came up and sat down next to her, rubbing his head against her side before plopping down his furry body on her lap.

A lot had happened in the decade that Suny had been in Colorado. She had been a Lake Michigan girl who would get on her bike, hit the Kal-Haven Trail and end up in South Haven for the day. Perfectly content to walk along the beach. Being absorbed with the ebb and flow of the waves. If you would have told her that she would wind up living in the foothills of the Rockies, she would have laughed.

But here she was. Decked out in shorts that covered her calves, thick socks tucked into hiker's boots to offer protection from ticks. Chestnut brown hair practically cut short so as not to interfere with the pottery process. In the place of warm sand under her feet Suny had discovered the beauty of the mountains. The first time she came across a herd of deer in the valley nearest her home, it was like a religious experience, for her, roughly the equivalent of ecstatic experiences recorded by the mystics.

This reverie was taking place on Saturday morning, when Suny could count on her mother, who still lived in Grand Junction, giving her a call. So her cell phone ringing didn't startle her.

"So, honey, how's your day going?"

"Hasn't really started yet, Mom." (Suny's mom could never quite understand the time zone difference.)

"I am so sorry! Did I wake you up again?"

"Don't worry about it. I'm having my coffee." (Suny had learned to set the coffee timer for 5:40 so that she'd at least have the benefit of waking up to fresh brewed as she was working her way through an early morning conversation.)

"The sky is such a lovely shade of robin's egg today. Absolutely gorgeous." It was her mom who had taught Suny that colors had hues and there was a continuum of colors that blended so beautifully into each other. Her mom was a freelance journalist, covering township news. The cost of living in Grand Junction was not that high, and she supplemented her income with other freelance work and actually made a good living at it. From her mom, Suny had learned how to use her creative talent to support herself while finding a small town to set up shop.

"How's the potter's wheel doing, honey?"

By now the coffee was kicking in, which was a good thing, because Suny was able to think through what she was going to say before it actually came out of her mouth.

"Well, it's funny that you mentioned robin's egg, Mom, because I've been experimenting a bit."

"How so?"

"I'm working on the opposite end of the spectrum, a deep, deep blue that's solid but translucent."

"I'd love to see it!"

"I can take a photo and send it to you. But it's hard to capture it without seeing it in natural light, you know? Sometimes the most enjoyable part of the process isn't the clay, it's developing the glaze. But then, you get to working on the wheel and your hands just guide you across the clay and they show you a double curve or a notch and that's gorgeous too."

"Sweetie, you're talking like a person in love with her work."

"Yeah, I guess so."

"Speaking of being in love…" (Suny's mom would sooner or

later get around to the subject of relationships. Not in the context of romance, but in terms of being human.) "How's it going in the friendship department?"

It had been almost two decades since Suny first set foot in Colorado, but she had yet to procure a best friend or even someone she could regularly confide in. Not that she didn't want to, but good friends weren't like a piece of pottery. You couldn't just throw a friendship back on the wheel if it wasn't forming right. If you got to the point where you could put it in the kiln, it could still blow up. And if that weren't enough, there were two totally distinct people involved, each one with their own history and expectations and ways of emotional expression. Just way too complicated to sustain.

"Mom, I'm doing ok."

"I'm sure you are, honey, but I'm a little concerned about your getting out and meeting people." (Suny's mom had a Midwesterner's vision of the West. Her being of the generation of "Gunsmoke" didn't help things any. According to 1960's American television, everyone out West had at least three friends – the sheriff, the saloon hall girl and a sidekick.)

"Don't worry Mom. I'll send you a picture of myself with some friends on Harley's this week, ok?" Around this point in the conversation, Suny's mom realized that she wasn't the one to preach to anyone about friendship. She knew almost everyone in Grand Junction, due to her newspaper work. But outside of those networkings, she really didn't have much of a social circle. (When Suny was three years old, her mom had come home from an interview in the middle of the afternoon to write up the story and found her husband had cleared out his portion of the bedroom closet and taped a fairly to-the-point note of explanation onto the closet door: "No offense intended, it's as much my fault as yours, but don't you think this is pretty boring?" She never heard from him again.)

C'est la vie, right?

"I'll talk with you later, sweetheart."

"Same time, same station. We're on Mountain Standard, Mom, ok?"

"Love you, sweetie!"

Suny set Buddy back down on the ground before getting up out of her chair. He stretched out completely, arching his back and shoving his head forward. She lay down her coffee cup and smiled at him. One of the side benefits of having a longhair was that when you picked him up and stroked him it was like holding a bunch of velvet that was alive and purring.

She would have been content to spend another hour or two sitting in the sun with him, but she wanted to get to the Farmer's Market early enough to get a good spot and get settled in.

As luck would have it, Suny wound up setting up next to Clive Morgenson, the guy who ran the CSA she belonged to. The name of his farm was Running Wild Greens. It was 20 acres of immaculately kept farmland, mostly given to lettuce, radishes, kale, bok choy, tomatoes and squash. Clive also put in some green beans, strawberries and herbs, mainly because no one else wanted to fiddle with high-maintenance crops. But he provided jobs, small as they were, by reaching out to the local middle school. Field trips given over to hands-on agriculture and during harvest time, the kids got to market and keep the proceeds from their work. Not a bad deal, he figured, and it pleased him to know he was doing his part to promote interest in local food among young kids.

That particular morning Clive had an array of greens along with first pickings of herbs. As usual he wasn't alone at his stall. There were three students from Hackett School there with him to gain experience with the retail end of things.

And, as usual, he was the one to initiate the conversation with Suny.

"Morning sleepyhead!" (In point of fact, Suny was by now thoroughly wide-awake and raring to go. Even if her mom hadn't called, by nature, she was an early morning person.)

"Yeah, well, which one of us has our mom on the phone at five in the morning each Saturday?"

"Try these," said Clive as he handed over a handful of strawberries. He knew that they happened to be Suny's favorite of all the earlier fruits, especially when they were warm and fresh picked. For a guy, Clive had his moments. For instance, he noticed that the blue in the pattern of the flannel shirt Suny was wearing perfectly matched her eyes. But of course he didn't mention it. He figured, why would a smart, gorgeous woman in her early 40's want anything to do with a short, slightly balding guy in his late 50's? Such a pair up might make for an interesting "older guy gets supremely lucky and meets an extremely attractive younger woman" type of movie, but that sort of thing didn't happen so much in real life. And anyway, Clive didn't think of Suny in a romantic sort of way, which was probably why they got along so well.

"Ohmygosh! They are soooo good!" Suny shot a spontaneous smile his way. "Absolutely heaven!"

"Well they ought to be!" said one of the middle-schoolers. "Mr. Morgenson treats those plants like they were his relatives or something."

"Yeah," spoke up the second middle-schooler. "For instance, did you know that every year you have to re-plant the runners and pull up older plants or the strawberries won't be as juicy? It's a real pain. But, actually, now that I think about it, it's worth the effort."

"You should get some of the strawberry jam over there," said the third middle-schooler. "It's more expensive than store-bought, but believe me, it's like ten times as flavorful."

"I'll consider it," said Suny, who had to admit she hadn't even noticed anything other than the greens and berries.

"So, how goes it Suny?" Clive asked, stretching as he spoke.

"Oh you know, the usual."

Clive tipped his cap back and laughed out loud at her answer.

"What's so funny!"

"Well, it sounds like..."

"... it sounds like you're in a restaurant ordering up your life," said the middle-schooler who had mentioned the runners, whose name was Jessie.

Yeah, it *does* sound like my life is pretty routine, thought Suny. Good heavens, here I am a Midwesterner transplanted in the foothills of some of the most gorgeous mountains on the face of the earth, fortunate enough to be working at something that is extremely creative, surrounded by so much beauty that I should hardly be able to stand it, but I don't feel that way.

"Sorry," she apologized. "That's not really what I meant at all."

"Excuse me, but yes it is," shot back the middle-schooler who had mentioned that Clive treated his plants like family. "In my experience, the first thing that comes out of a person's mouth is what they're truly feeling. Now, if Mr. Morgenson was asking you something about mathematics or quantum physics or logarithms or something like that, it would be a different story, but he isn't, so I definitely agree. My name's Trenton." And for some reason he felt like he should stick out his hand by way of a formal introduction.

"Pleased to meet you, Trenton, but I must respectfully disagree with your analysis."

"If people just told the truth, life would be a whole lot simpler," said the middle-schooler who had mentioned the jam. Her name was Samantha, and she had set up quite a system for differentiating among people who knew her. Close friends called her Sam by invitation only. Others whom she felt comfortable enough with called her Sammy, sort of as an on-the-way-to-possible-good-friends designation. Family members called her Sam-oh, which really wasn't her fault. Her dad, a notorious practical joker, had dubbed her Sam-oh two days after she got home after being born because of the way she curled her mouth into an "o" shape when she was pondering the universe in front of her, which she did quite a lot.

"Her name's Samantha," explained Clive. "But depending upon how the morning goes, you may wind up calling her Sammy, or possibly Sam-oh."

Samantha arched her eyebrows and looked Suny straight on. "I doubt very seriously that it'll change from Samantha to anything else today. I don't mean to offend you, but I don't make important decisions like that hastily."

"She's right," Clive corrected himself. "I've known Samantha for two years now, and I still haven't broken into the inner circle."

As if to emphasize the point that there were no hard feelings behind her factual statement, Samantha offered Suny another handful of strawberries.

"Thank you, Samantha. No hard feelings then?"

"Absolutely not. Life's too short. By the way, I really like your shirt. The blue in the pattern perfectly matches your eyes, which are drop dead beautiful by the way. Don't you agree, Mr. Morgenson?"

Clive, caught unawares, spat out the blueberry-pomegranate juice he was drinking which had gone down the wrong way, ushering in a few coughs to clear the airway.

Jessie picked up the conversation at this point. "Mr. Morgenson only coughs like that when something or someone makes him nervous. You should pay attention to that if you want to get to know him more than as a farmer's market stall-mate. Unless you're into being a nun."

Trenton, who had a reputation among the ladies as being sort of dense, and feeling obligated to defend his male friend, spoke up: "Women! They don't seem to know a good thing when they've got it!"

Although Suny was technically a mostly-lapsed Protestant, and had traded tradition and hierarchy for a more personal relationship with the Eternal One, she was intrigued with the tail end of Jesse's comment.

"I'm afraid the sisterhood never really appealed to me."

"Nowadays there are tons of experimental ways of living

out spiritual commitments communally," explained Jessie. "But I was focusing on Mr. Morgenson and your relationship with him, not on becoming a nun."

"Whoa now!" It was Clive's moment to re-enter the conversation. "Guys, I appreciate your enthusiasm, but I don't need your help ok?"

"No offense Mr. Morgenson, but I'm going to go out on a limb and guess that you should have asked Suny out on a date ages ago."

"It's the whole can't-get-past-first-base thing, Mr. M," said Jessie, casting an eye towards Suny. "I mean, she's obviously interested in you.

"Like I said, guys, thanks for the effort, but I don't need your assistance. Suny and I are friends. That's it."

"Right!" Suny was too quick to respond.

"Then why are you so nervous?" asked Jessie. "Or does the thought of selling your pottery usually make you so anxious?"

Clive let out another laugh and shook his head before turning to Suny. "Sorry, if I'd known that these guys were charter members of Matchmakers Anonymous, I wouldn't have invited them here today."

'Hey, I'm not interested in fixing you two up," argued Trenton. "Although, I'll be the first to admit that you do make a great looking couple."

"Way to ruin the mood!" said Samantha as she nudged Trenton so hard that he almost fell over frontwards.

"Listen up. There is no mood here!" This time Clive actually sounded a bit irritated by the whole thing.

But Suny wasn't so eager to back him up. She looked at Trenton intently: "Really, you think we look good together?"

"Absolutely."

Not content to let the proverbial sleeping dog lie, she asked the same question to Jessie and Samantha. "How about you? What's your opinion?"

"I already told you how Mr. M feels about you," said Jessie.

"If you feel the same, then it's a green light situation as far as I can see it."

Suny said nothing and arched her eyebrows towards Samantha, giving her permission to speak her mind.

"I agree. In my experience men never are straight with expressing their emotions when it comes to romance. They get nervous and then they get scared and then they start lying like crazy."

Now Suny nudged Clive, hoping to good naturedly coax him into a statement on the subject. "Well, let's see. Yeah, I think boys in middle school still have a lot of emotional growing up to do. And while they're doing it, as far as relationships with the opposite sex go, they do tend to skip around the truth a bit."

"A bit?!" said Samantha. "A bit? That's like saying that camels tend to drink a smidgen of water out there in the desert. When it comes to relationships, boys lie, case closed. It's buried deep inside their DNA so they aren't even aware of it. A guy will tell a girl that he's madly in love with her when they're alone, and two seconds later in the hallway at school he'll be joking about the same girl with his buddies like she means absolutely nothing, because he's a guy and has to look cool with his so-called peers. But when it gets reported back to his girlfriend, he'll deny it to her face, point blank. Tell me that isn't schizo!"

"One of us just broke up with her boyfriend," offered Jessie, casting a sympathetic eye towards Samantha.

"It happens every day," replied Trenton. "Fact of life. Only guys don't get all upset over it."

"That's all well and good," said Jessie, "but actually we were trying to determine what Mr. M felt towards Suny before we got majorly sidetracked. So, what about it Mr. M?"

Clive took off his cap, ran his hand through what was left of his hair and adjusted his glasses.

"There are some subjects that just aren't appropriate topics for general discussion."

"Like what?" asked Trenton, who was immediately nudged in the ribs from both sides by Jessie and Samantha.

Turning to face Suny directly, Clive continued: "But I'd like to invite the subject of this interrogation to dinner. That is, if she's free and interested."

Suny's face exploded into a wide grin. "I am, and I am!"

"Smooth!" whispered Trenton.

"Spoken like a true gentleman," said Jessie, nodding her approval.

Samantha handed Suny another handful of strawberries.

"Thank you Samantha!"

"It's Sam-oh," she corrected.

For Emily

This was Dominic's fifth mission trip to Northern Ireland. He was helping a reconciliation group headed up by a husband and wife, based in the village of Darkley. Though most of County Armagh was rural, even Darkley qualified as being a dot on a map. It was an old linen mill town, consisting of one street with maybe 45 row houses strung together at a top of a hill. There was a post office which shared a building with the abandoned remains of what had long ago been a grocer's. The nearest school was in Keady, three miles down the road. Although Darkely was a Catholic village, the closest church, two miles away across a rolling hill, was Mountain Lodge. It was a Protestant congregation, five of whose elders had been gunned down during a Sunday evening service during the height of The Troubles. If you looked carefully, you could still see the pock marked sanctuary wall.

The place where Dominic stayed when helping out Dermid and Jeanenne was the former mansion of the linen mill owner. (There had been a long history of oppression of Irish workers by English mill owners.) Dermid used to say that it was poetic justice that what had once been a source of suffering and suppression was now being used as the headquarters to bring God's love to a place desperately in need of it.

The normal flow of the week devoted to kids outreach in July was simple. The focus was engaging the kids living in a housing estate, with a series of songs and dramas and games that would get them away from thinking of God in terms of Catholic and Protestant. Broadening the mind in hopes of dissolving the prejudice was the key.

At the end of this week of outreach, the tradition with Dermid and Jeanenne was to host a barbeque for all the volunteers. This particular year the celebration was being held in the home of Kathleen and Jesse. Kathleen was a spirited Irish girl, with bright red hair and blue eyes the color of the Irish Sea on a good day. Jesse was a tall, handsome man who had the build of a farmer but the sensitivity of an elementary school teacher, which he was. Kathleen and Jesse were part of the outreach team and loved to open up their home.

For Dominic it was going to be a bittersweet evening because he was extremely sentimental and wasn't really looking forward to the separation from the friends he had made over the years. It was a grand dinner, with chicken, burgers, mashed potatoes, and a salad, with red wine. Dominic wasn't used to drinking and one glass of the wine had washed away his normal inhibitions. The wine worked its magic, in part, because of the atmosphere of Ireland, where despite the religious prejudice, there remained a spirit of hospitality that induced story-telling and lingering on into the wee hours.

At one point, Dermid got up and thanked the assembled volunteers, maybe a dozen in all, for their help. He encouraged them to remember that God was bigger than religion. Then Jeanenne got up and introduced Emily. "I've got a surprise for everyone," she said. "Even though Emily hasn't been part of our team this year, she was keen on coming tonight to play some music for us."

So saying, Jeanenne kissed her husband, shot Dominic a wry smile and sat down. Emily got up, headed towards the piano, seated herself and began to play. From the moment her hands hit the keyboard, Dominic was transfixed.

"Who is this woman?" he asked Jeanenne.

Jeanenne raised her eyebrows, "Why don't you ask her yourself?"

Emily's playing was smooth and deep and filled the room with warmth. Her hands flew across the keyboard and at points she arched her back, letting her black hair fall across her shoulders, as she gave in to the music. Dominic wasn't normally partial to the piano, but he found himself completely taken.

And he was astonished after Emily finished playing when she calmly got up and walked, very slowly, across the room and sat down next to him.

"Hello," she said, holding out her hand.

"That was absolutely brilliant."

"Thanks."

"How long have you been playing?"

"I don't. I mean, not for public consumption anyway." Then she laughed.

Now right here would be a good a place as any to mention that this isn't going to be one of those typical Irish stories where someone from America comes over to Ireland and it's always sunny and near the sea and they meet a local native who is absolutely beautiful or handsome. And the person from Ireland is really down to earth and lives in a small village but the person from America is sharp and cynical because they were recently dumped by someone who was engaged to them.

Or else it's always raining and near a castle where long ago a beautiful townsperson fell in love with a handsome high king and they were about to run away together, but the beautiful townsperson became ill with consumption and died. Sort of like John Keats, but not nearly as lyrical. Anyway, of course the high king became extremely distressed and couldn't take living in the castle anymore, so he left. Leaving a castle (which stood along a bluff on the sea), to depreciate into ruins. Then two hundred years later another person from America, usually a sharp-eyed man, comes over on business only to fall in love with the village tour guide when she forces him to hike up to the castle against his will.

And this also isn't going to be the sort of Irish story in which a great-uncle of an American dies with no children, leaving only a beautiful great niece with thick wavy hair as sole inheritor. Of course the great-niece, whose name is Megan and lives in Boston or Chicago, immediately drops everything and takes the next plane to a small Irish village that also has a castle near it. Only this time, the castle is the home of the great-uncle and the will is to be read there. So once in the village, Megan has to enlist the help of McMurphy, the proprietor of the local pub, who is also the barrister. As it turns out, Megan is absolutely gorgeous, funny, smart-as-a-whip and has a very distinct laugh. McMurphy, whose hair is also black and wavy, is somewhat reserved for an Irishman, but Megan is just the sort of girl who can loosen him up.

Speaking of loosening up, this most definitely isn't going to be one of those stories of an Irish guy who comes to New York City to get a loan from the Irish-American Society to start up a soccer club in his village back in Dundalk. This guy's name has to be Turley or James or Sean. Turns out, the person granting loans is a girl who graduated from City College. Her name is Colleen and she's Irish on both her parents' sides. But she's never been to Ireland. At first she thinks Turley or James or Sean is doing a good job spreading the blarney a bit too thick. She's a big-city girl after all and she doesn't know Dundalk from Detroit. And even though the Dundalk train station has all these lovely quotes about the romance of travel written on its walls, she's not buying any of it.

That is, until James or Sean or Turley challenges Colleen to come with him to Dundalk to see the town and realize for herself that he's legitimate. Ordinarily Colleen wouldn't flinch at such an offer, thinking it was complete rubbish. But there's something in Turley or James or Sean's green eyes that catches her attention, so off she goes. She and Turley or James or Sean have lots of time to chat and get to know each other on the Air Lingus flight. And when Colleen sees, first hand, all those romantic sayings written on the walls of the train station, she falls hopelessly in love on the spot.

And I'm really very sorry if you think this is the sort of Irish story that begins in Armagh outside the cinema. The movie playing is "500 Days of Summer," and even though the narrator warns the audience that "this is not a love story," it actually is. For Deven and Aberdeen, it's their first date. He works as a produce manager at Sainsbury's, and – God love us – she's an American in Armagh for the summer on a university exchange program tied to getting her master's in sociology. Deven's a highly excited, slightly neurotic guy who only wears his work uniform of white shirt and blue slacks. Which, under normal circumstances might make him fairly uninteresting, but he happens to look just like a young Dustin Hoffman, with Irish cuteness to boot. Aberdeen, in a cultural cross-type, is very laid back and a good cook.

And because the family she's staying with is out getting fish and chips, then visiting relatives in Portadown afterwards, she offers to have Deven over for supper. While she cooks, Deven spills his guts about how he has never dated in his life because his mom died when he was approaching puberty, leaving him incredibly insecure when it comes to women. In turn, Aberdeen confesses that (even though she looks like a young Elizabeth Taylor), she is actually quite shy around guys and has trouble getting dates. As always, the story ends with Deven and Aberdeen around the supper table, smiling at each other over wine, as Aberdeen feels free to get up and give Deven a kiss, promising the start of a brilliant relationship.

So, getting back to Emily and Dominic, Emily turned red after laughing and sat there staring at him.

"Are you ok?" he asked.

"Yes, sorry, I only meant that I'm not an accomplished pianist.

It helped that Dominic was not his usual uptight self. "Well, the way you play, it's mesmerizing."

Emily also played the Irish harp, but she didn't want to push the envelope just then by mentioning it. She had been playing since her roommate at University of Edinburgh introduced her to the instrument. She took lessons for four years at a place along the Royal Mile.

Emily loved Edinburgh, but she missed her family and even more, she missed being involved with her country. Northern Ireland was a mess and it broke her heart to see union jacks and IRA flags competing with each other at the entranceway to almost every town throughout Ulster, an embarrassing symbol of intolerance.

"So, you're part of Dermid and Jeanenne's crew then?"

"Sort of. I'm summer help."

Dominic wanted to explain how he became involved. How one day, out of the blue, he picked up a stack of books on Irish history at the public library and was instantly captivated. Even though he hadn't a drop of Irish blood in his body, he could relate to the religious tension in the North coming from a family where his father was Roman Catholic, but his mom was a Methodist.

"So you're one of those Americans who aims to save us from our worst self?"

Emily couldn't help but smile again as she inched a little closer to Dominic. Although she didn't know him at all, she could see Jeanenne and Dermid both nodding their approval and any friend of theirs was also hers. She knew that Dermid had paid a dear price for the ministry he had chosen in Crossmaglen, more than 25 years past. Initially he had gone door-to-door introducing himself as neither Catholic nor Protestant but simply a follower of Jesus. The effect had been doors slammed in his face, and he learned to keep his handkerchief at hand to wipe away the spittle let fly for emphasis.

Emily's brown eyes were extremely sympathetic and kind. (She was the daughter of a carpenter, Ian, whose work was widely respected for its quality.) Emily had grown up in a loving family where opinions were given openly and respected. Her mother, Madigan, was one of five siblings whose parents were also uncharacteristically open-minded and charitable. Neither family had chosen to send their children to the local public schools, but home schooled them as best they could away from parochial short-sightedness. These were the days before free schools offered an option to the public system.

"Not really," Dominic responded. "I don't have any Irish in me, but I'm sympathetic to the cause. It pains me to see people putting religion above relationship with God. And I love working with kids."

"Me too. Besides which, I've got a great job working as a veterinarian. There still aren't that many female vets in County Armagh, so I get to preach the gospel by default when I go on calls. Farmers take their livestock seriously, so when I come they're naturally in a frame of mind to chat about the Almighty. And the fact that I'm a woman totally disarms them."

"It's not 'All Creatures Great and Small' then?"

"Not by a long shot."

Before the night was over, Emily and Dominic were well on their way towards a friendship. Shortly after Dermid mouthed the words: "You can trust him," to Emily, she asked Dominic if he would like to spend a day with her making rounds before he left Darkley for America. It was decided that the most practical thing to do was gather his things and let Emily take him to the flat she had above the clinic.

It was only an hour's trip away. After a pot of tea was shared, Dominic rolled out a thick duvet that Emily had given him on the couch and promptly fell asleep. The next morning, after a breakfast of oatmeal and toast, Emily checked in downstairs to get her calls for the day.

"I've got three tuberculosis inoculations lined up and need to check in with a farmer whose cow is in the family way."

By mid-morning the inoculations were behind them and as

Emily was turning her car into the driveway of her last call, she was met by the farmer.

"You're a sight for sore eyes!"

"How's that?"

"She's about ready to blow. Over there in the barn. Been mooing like mad."

Emily parked the car, and turned to Dominic. "So how are you with the sight of blood?"

"I've worked as an in-take clerk in emergency rooms back home."

"Okay. then, how about poo?"

"What do you mean?"

Emily got her kit out of the boot of the car and pointed to a bucket and a hose. "Can you fill this up with water please?"

"Who's he?" asked the anxious farmer.

"Relax, Arlen, he's a medical friend of mine. Just show me to the mommy to be."

The cow was standing up in the barn facing the door, so Emily suggested that they bring her out in the open for some fresh air to begin with. Besides, it would be easier to conduct an exam in the light.

As Dominic came back with the bucket of water, Emily already had her arms, up to her elbows, stuck up the cow's back end.

"The calf's head is caught around the umbilical cord, hold on. I can feel it."

Within ten very nerve-wracking minutes, Emily had successfully turned the calf's head enough to unwind the cord from it. With all the stimulation, the cow was more than ready to give birth.

"Come on baby, push now!" coaxed Emily, "you can do this! I know you're ready for the wee one to come out."

Then she turned to Dominic. "When the calf's out, after I cut the cord, please wash the wee one down. The mom's going to be too exhausted to do it."

Ten minutes later, after much pulling, the delivery was complete. Emily sat on her haunches, catching her breath, her arms completely covered in poo. "When you're done with the calf, could you please get another bucket for me?"

By now you've probably realized that this isn't going to be the sort of Irish story where an American businessman from Boston is considering closing down a fishery in Portavogie because the company is consolidating and can't afford to keep it operating. He sends David, his assistant, there to tell them the bad news. In the meantime, the entire village gets wind of it and enlists Mary Maeye, the daughter of Ennis, the elder statesman of the village, to make a plea to David.

Initially, David is all business, and only dresses in three piece suits and proper shoes. Completely unfit to walk around town. Over a lunch of fish and chips, Mary Maeve convinces him he'd have more success meeting with the locals if he attempted to dress like one. So she goes with him to Dougal's Finery where David purchases jeans and an Aryan wool sweater that perfectly complements his salt-and-pepper hair and brown eyes. Meanwhile, Mary Maeve gets herself invited to dinner at the bed and breakfast where David is staying the evening before the big meeting with the town council. The one where he's going to drop the bomb on them.

But during dinner, David notices that the candlelight is dancing in Mary Maeve's gorgeous eyes and because she's wearing a brown wool rag sweater with blue overtones, he can't decide if her eyes are hazel or grey. As Mary Maeve leans forward to tell him, he drinks in her perfume, and realizes that he can't tell the town council that he's closing the fishery because he's in love.

Dominic came back with the bucket of water and spoke as Emily made a move to put her arms into it.

"Here, let me wash you. It'll save water."

Emily was impressed with the gentleness and thoroughness of the washing.

"Now I know what you meant by the poo remark."

"Sorry about that. You have to love poo to be a vet."

They both laughed. By the time Emily had said good-bye to a much-relieved Arlen, it was time for dinner.

"I know of a great Chinese place back in town," she suggested. Dominic was for it.

Now, you might be thinking: This isn't one of those Irish stories, that after dinner Emily drops Dominic off at the train station without a chance to chat. Or maybe having great Chinese food helped Dominic further relax to the point where he could fully appreciate that a woman like Emily doesn't come around but once in a lifetime.

But what actually happened was this: It was dark out after dinner. Emily and Dominic walked to her car and she drove him all the way back to Darkley.

Emily was in no hurry to say good-bye. In fact, when they pulled into the driveway, she led Dominic up a hill in back of the mansion where Dermid and Jeannene lived. It was a high place and you could easily see two miles away in daylight.

Dominic began the conversation. "I've really enjoyed today."

Emily nodded. "So, did you notice we're standing behind a full moon?"

Dominic turned around and saw it was absolutely gorgeous, having just risen in the sky. "In all the times I've been in the North, I've never been outside at night to see one."

"Did you know we've got a tradition in Armagh about the full moon?"

Emily inched, every so slightly, closer to Dominic and looked deep into his eyes. Dominic smiled in response. Then he asked her to explain what the tradition was. So Emily leaned into him, whispering: "If you kiss someone for the first time under a full moon, you'll fall in love."

And they did.

CPSIA information can be obtained at www.ICGtesting.com
Printed in the USA
LVOW07s1949290714

396583LV00001B/84/P

9 781490 805801